Nyifie Brothers Publishing

ANARCHY AND BLOOD

THE VAMPIRE MAURICE (A FAT VAMPIRE SIDE SERIES) - BOOK 2

JOHNNY B. TRUANT

ONE
DEAD AGAIN

Dr. Annabel Rice sat right leg over left, crossed at the knee, in sensible slacks because male patients sometimes tried to look up skirts. Her notepad was on her lower thigh, heel of her right hand on its pages, a black Cross pen hovering above the paper. She was trying very hard not to tap the pen or bounce her crossed-over leg. Usually she didn't have a problem with fidgeting when her patients went quiet. This one was different, unnerving her enough to fuss. Whenever Maurice stopped talking, she kept wanting to poke him just to make sure he wasn't dead.

Which he was, of course.

The thought gave Annabel a chill, and it was already cold in here. She'd donned her blazer after shaking Maurice's hand, hiding her surprise that her new vampire patient had returned for a second session. His skin was like matte ice. It had a way of sucking the heat from the room.

A wall clock, just out of sight, counted the seconds.

Tick.

Tick.

When Maurice looked away, Annabel leaned back to

spy the clock. It was 7:07. Less than ten minutes wasted, but it felt like an eternity. Getting paid for nothing was nice, but her unease kept building. Usually she liked to outlast quiet, but this time required intervention.

"I'll be honest," Annabel said. "I wasn't sure you'd come back."

"We had an appointment, didn't we?"

"People miss appointments. You wouldn't be the first."

"That's pretty rude."

Annabel's forehead wrinkled. She'd had a week to ponder the notion that she was now counseling a vampire, and strangely it'd sunk in fine. Maurice had done something to her mind at his first appointment: *glamouring*, they called it. Apparently glamour allowed Annabel to retain the knowledge she needed to treat him (namely that he was two thousand years old, nearly immortal, and drank blood to survive) without that knowledge upsetting her. Before Maurice, she hadn't known vampires existed. Now she did, and yet her life hadn't changed. Whatever mental gag he'd put on her had let her keep her wits. She hadn't dreamed of blood rites, sowed her windowsills with garlic, or even told her horrible husband. Or at least she *thought* she hadn't told him. For some reason the topic — as was true of many things about her husband, probably because he was an asshole — was foggy.

But hearing the vampire talk of rudeness? *That* was downright surreal.

"Rude, maybe," Annabel said. "But no-showing for an appointment could also be protective."

"Protecting whom?"

Whom, yet. Bram Stoker hadn't gotten the high-falutin' quite right.

"Themselves."

"People skip appointments to protect themselves from *you?*" He'd adopted a classic lay-down on the couch despite Annabel's note that most patients sat up and looked her in the eye. Saying this, though, he *did* sit up; he *did* look her in the eye. He seemed to be saying, ... *but you're not a threat. Why, I could rip you apart with one finger.* That gave her a chill, too.

She shifted.

"You're nervous."

"I'm not."

"Yes you are. You're freaking out right now. I'm not going to hurt you, you know."

Yeah, well, this fear wasn't a conscious thing. It was instinctual, the way prey fears even domesticated predators.

"Please don't read my mind," Annabel said.

"I'm not. I'm reading your body language."

"But you *could* read my mind, if you wanted to."

"Human minds are very hard to read. We can glamour you, even control you. We can make you remember or forget. But we can only see into the minds of other vampires, and only if we're related to them."

"'*Very hard* to read humans.' But it's possible."

"Maybe under extraordinary circumstances."

"And it's possible to read other vampire minds, even if you're not related."

Maurice nodded, catching her reference to last time's story: the 1920s, the Vampire Mafia, and most of all Daisy.

"Extenuating circumstances."

"Because of Thrilloglobin. The drug."

"Not at all." Now Maurice sat up proper. He was curious, reading her face again. "That's not the first time you asked about Thrill," he said.

"Yes it is."

"You said something right when I came in."

"Maurice, I didn't."

He was squinting again. Now she was unsure. If she'd asked when he'd first arrived, she didn't remember. But why *would* she ask? Thrilloglobin was synthetic blood, a drug for them, irrelevant to humans. Still ... maybe she had? She'd been forgetful the whole week — enough that she'd wondered what was amiss. If it wasn't Maurice's glamour that was giving her blackouts, what was? It's not like she knew any other vampires. It was just Annabel, her husband, and the neighbors she also didn't like. Domestic life kind of sucked. No wonder she was losing time — anything to get away from the douchebags.

"Doesn't matter, I guess," she said.

Maurice laid back down. Sixty quiet seconds passed.

"So is that it?" Annabel asked when the minute was over.

"Is *what* it?"

"You came all the way down here, then laid on the couch and looked at my ceiling. Other than hello and our discussion just now, you haven't said a word. Are you going to speak? At all?"

"Am I supposed to?"

"I'm your doctor, Maurice. *You* came to *me*. I can't glamour like you can. If you want me to know what's in your head, you have to tell me."

A voice inside Annabel's head — one she barely recognized — added a P.S. to that: *But it won't be that way forever.*

Maurice was looking at her again.

"Are you okay?"

"I'm fine."

"You seem tired."

"I haven't been sleeping well. My husband …" But she trailed off. What had she been about to say?

"Yes?"

Annabel barely heard. She was trying to recall, coming up empty. Forgetful again: finally losing her mind under the weight of everyone else's problems. She looked like shit, too. Applying makeup this morning had been like using spackle to repair a crumbling dam. Eventually she'd given up on looking okay and settled instead for dusting the bags under her eyes, trying to embrace the ugly.

"Let's talk about you, Maurice," Annabel said. "Are *you* okay?"

"I'm fine."

"Do you have any thoughts about our last session? First time seeing a psychiatrist in a life as long as yours … it has to have stirred something."

He shifted, uncomfortable: *Bullseye.*

"It has, hasn't it?" she asked.

"Isn't this supposed to be self-directed? You say nothing other than 'Mmm-hmm' while I say whatever comes to mind?"

"Not since Freud."

"So what kind of therapy *do* you use, Dr. Rice? What school of thought?"

She just stared at him, calling him on stalling without saying a word.

Finally he settled back and crossed his arms. "All right. Truth is, it's like our last session cracked my brain open. My thoughts won't sit still. I've got a lot of thoughts, you know."

"Tell me one."

"I keep thinking about the past. I've always just done things, but now I keep wondering if they were the *right* things."

"Retrospection. That's healthy."

"Is it? I'm not sure I like who I've been."

"That's a common refrain with you. Last time, you worried that you're too selfish. Now you're second-guessing your past. I know that can be scary, but it's all growth."

"What if it's just doubt?"

"Even doubt is *awareness*. Seeing yourself and your actions clearly is what matters. Most people don't really think about what they do. Thinking about those things at all — even if you don't like what you see — is progress."

"I suppose."

"The best strategy is just to keep looking. Keep examining your past with open eyes and minds."

Maurice shrugged. "It's such a long life. Where do I begin?"

"Usually I'd say to start with your parents, but do you even remember yours?"

Now Maurice was the one to shrug: *Not really. Not at all.*

"Your maker, then." She had an idea. "Or your *wife*."

"Celeste?"

"Why not? She sounds like an anchor to you. Yin and yang, maybe. Am I close?"

"I suppose you could say she completes me?" He sounded like he was joking, but Annabel knew discomfort when she heard it.

"And you've been with her for a millennium. So anything you've seen or experienced or done — even things that bother you — have been done with her by your side. Or ... without her *leaving* your side."

"And?"

"Well, how bad can your worst transgressions be — how

selfish — if Celeste has stuck with you through thick and thin?"

Maurice's mouth worked. She knew she'd hit another bullseye. Or perhaps stepped on a landmine.

"What if," he said, "there were times Celeste *wasn't* with me?"

Annabel recrossed her legs, now tapping her pen on the pad despite her best intentions.

"Tell me," she said.

TWO

LONER

When you're immortal, you go through life crises just to mark the time. Humans turn forty and buy a sports car or get plastic surgery or take up a youthful new hobby, suddenly aware that they've been dangling above a great existential pit all along. Vampires, on the other hand, never know when we've hit "mid-life." We might live a human lifespan and end up staked, or we might live ten thousand years and finally walk into the sun out of boredom. At 200, are you old? Or is 200 barely old enough to have the equivalent of teen angst — rebelling and acting out like a kid?

What humans forget about vampires is that at the end of the day, we're ultimately just people.

Celeste and I have been married for almost a thousand years. We do pretty well, but anyone is bound to have a few disagreements over the course of a millennium. We've always been in and out, up and down. Sometimes we're like kids in love and sometimes eternity feels like a very long time. We don't like to talk about it — Celeste in particular — because when we reconcile, it always feels inevitable. Time apart has always, even in the moment, felt like exactly that:

time apart. Never have we separated with more than the intention to take a break.

Historically, it's always been me who pulls away. Either I come down with a plague of wanderlust or I act like an asshole for long enough that Celeste kicks me out. In the end — and this, I think, proves my point — our separations have always been The Maurice Show. It happens because I want more than I have. It happens when something good suddenly isn't good enough, and I go looking for more. Vampire lust to the core, I suppose: our species's penchant for gluttony. Or at least my own.

In 1985, I was off on one such bender. I'd lived through the '60s, when all my human meals tasted like kush and their blood made my vampire mind try to go on strange drug trips. I'd lived through the '70s, when it seemed like the whole world had lost the desire to bathe and shave. By the time the '80s hit and greed grew popular again, the change was welcome. But although it's obvious now, I didn't realize at the time that I was homing in on the "Me" of the "Me Decade." It felt quite the opposite.

I've talked about how I left France because I was tired of the pomp and circumstance abroad — and after that mess in the '20s, I was tired of America, too. The '30s, '40s, and '50s were a reaction to the thing with Daisy and the Vampire Mafia, and I don't remember *living* those decades so much as just trying to *get through* them. We somehow learned to move on after Daisy and the Mafia never bothered us again. Still, it felt like thirty years of drift. I got disillusioned — probably very lost. The '60s and '70s, as much as I complained about humans then, were the decades in which I finally relaxed. And by "relaxed," I mean that I rolled with the culture, though Celeste and I kept ourselves away from it. We turned on, tuned in, and dropped out.

Apathy became the watchword. I told myself I was chill. Actually, I was more tense than ever.

But then the '80s hit. Pac-Man was released, John Lennon got murdered, Richard Pryor set himself on fire, and everyone wanted to know who shot J.R. The world gave us *E.T.* and Tony Hawk and IBM computers. Humans, exhausted from trying to care about an entire Earth, seemed to give up and care about nothing but their wardrobes. Even the drugs changed; I tasted it in their blood. Humans smoked less weed, which was social, and did more coke, which was solo. And I could *do* solo. I did the '80s so well — got *so good* at feeding my surface-level pleasures the moment they arrived — that Celeste and I started to fight. I told her I needed space. I wasn't a '70s cuddler; I was an '80s individualist. She kicked my ass out and off I went, declaring good riddance. I didn't need her. Hell, I didn't need *anyone.*

So I struck out on my own: wandering, seeing how far an all-night bus would take me. I ended up in Texas, which didn't suit me, then its capital of Austin, which did. Just as the 1930s were a counter-reaction to the 1920s for me, so was Austin a counter-reaction to Oklahoma. Oklahoma was full of good ol' boys, and they didn't diminish once I was in the Lone Star state. I was at a bus station in some little burg after midnight, ready to take any route that'd remove me from all the hats, spurs, and classic values, when I met my tribe.

Punks. On haj, to the city where they kept things weird.

I figured, *Hey, I'm basically a punk. I believe in chaos and anarchy; I don't play by anyone else's rules; I'm anti-establishment on two separate continents. I don't play well with others unless they, too, don't play well with others. I'm single, I'm wild, I'm young at heart, and I tend to seriously fuck shit up.*

Besides, I'd been high-class before and was sick of it. I was ready for something new — something trashy and on-the-streets. In the '80s, you either were "The Man" or you rallied against him. And now here, right in front of me, were some weirdly-dressed, crass assholes who were very much *against.* People who'd left it all behind, like I had, to rage against the machine.

So I got on the bus, and joined them.

THREE
SUBVERTISING

The big light hit us and Jess yelled, *"BOOK!"*

Which, given our circumstances, wasn't easy. Jess was on the next building as lookout, just two flights from the ground past all those nudie calendars ... but the others were on the same rooftop as me, not nearly as mobile. Anarchy Jim was in a DIY rope harness with spray cans and a stencil. Stacy Grace was belaying him so he didn't die. Watlin, for some reason, was eating the hot fudge cake he'd grabbed at a Big Boy while the others were buying smokes. Looking at Watlin, you'd never know anything was wrong. He was wearing a sweater vest, hair combed and perfect, looking absurd levels of normal. Watlin, at least, was calm as a cucumber. Everyone else was running. It took all my restraint not to leap three stories to the street when the cops showed up.

Apparently, we were criminals.

Apparently someone around town had been vandalizing billboards and wallside advertisements in clever, inspired ways. Apparently, the Austin Police had a file.

Apparently, the cops had tracked the undesirables behind the vandalism to just off-campus, east side of 35, maybe along the Drag. Drag worms, the cops knew, were transient at best, street litter at worst. They'd sell out anyone to avoid a bust. I found it insulting; people called the Drag worms "punks" when they clearly weren't, when they were bums or rich kids slumming it, living on the street for a change of pace. If the cops wanted to bust the *punks* responsible for all those clever subvertisements, they could at least stop conflating us with the goddamn worms. Drag worms were lazy without purpose. We, on the other hand, were lazy with a mission. "From the couch to the battlefield and back," Anarchy Jim liked to say. We ended up drunk and lethargic in the end, but at least we tried to change the world first.

"STAY WHERE YOU ARE," blared a megaphone.

Stacy, more impatient than flustered, dropped Jim the rest of the way to the rooftop. She'd lowered him twenty feet; the last five would have been coddling. I heard a thump, a grunt, and a whoosh of exhaled breath. Her burden handled, Stacy turned and hauled ass down the staircase. She'd been raised on the streets; I knew she'd be fine. If caught, she'd scam her way out of arrest. Or, knowing Stacy, she might just punch the cops in the dick. Not kick — *punch*. Years later, I'm pretty sure they copied Stacy's signature move for the video game *Bad Dudes*.

"COME DOWN FROM THE ROOF. DO NOT TRY AND RUN."

My eye caught Roland down below, running with a fat officer huffing behind.

Anarchy Jim was at my shoulder.

"Down the fire escape, dude" he said. "Hurry."

But Watlin was still where he'd been, eating hot fudge cake with a plastic fork. Did he even know the cops were here? Watlin, as mainstream he looked, had always been the weirdest of us.

It seemed that Jim was only selfless enough to make the suggestion, not to wait for me to take it. When I paused, he shoved past me. There were two squad cars below us, their blue-and-reds throwing disco lights on the intersection opposite. I thought Jim had a good chance of making it; both cars were on the wrong side of the building. Who were these guys — trainees? It's as if they thought we'd just *freeze* when told to. Not used to punks, I guess.

"Watlin!"

He looked up. Chocolate on his lip.

"*The cops!*"

"Hot fudge cake!"

I waved, urgent. The access door opened: the cops arriving. I heard myself say, *Shit*. We hadn't expected company. The roof was littered with things that could identify us: spraypaint, which we'd lifted from the auto shop where Stacy worked. The DIY harness: a belt with an Exploited buckle that Jim had made himself. Everyone knew the abandoned building we squatted in; all the cops would need to do was ask. With all the crap we were leaving behind, we might as well have been laying breadcrumbs.

But it wasn't the cops at the roof access stairs. It was Jess. She'd gone down, then up. That was Jess for you: moving into danger instead of running away.

"What's taking you guys so long?" she demanded.

I gathered the spraypaint and harness, then grabbed Watlin's sleeve and yanked him upright. Hot fudge cake hit the tar paper at our feet. Watlin gasped.

"Nothing," I told Jess. "Let's go."

From beneath us, the megaphone sounded again: "WE HAVE YOU SURROUNDED."

With the access door still open, we could hear footsteps. Cops, rushing up to greet us — for real this time.

"Where's Jim?" Jess asked.

"He's fine," I said.

"I don't care if he's fine. I care where he is."

Her eyes darted. She actually meant, ... *where he went.* She'd come up the stairs and hadn't run into Anarchy Jim, or maybe she'd crossed from the building opposite without going to ground, walking twenty feet through the construction framework between. Across the scaffolding, I saw, was a huge Fleur-de-Lis. Not the French icon — the logo of the construction company. Fleur-de-Lis Development had been reshaping Austin for a few years, it seemed, but we hadn't connected the dots until recently. The oversight, Jim had said in his righteous way, was egregious and unforgivable. If we'd pulled off this caper, we'd already planned to hit them next.

"He ran that way." I pointed. "Down the fire escape."

"STOP YOUR VANDALISM IMMEDIATELY. THIS IS THE POLICE."

"Does the guy with the megaphone think we don't know who's come to arrest us?" I asked.

Watlin stood beside me, waiting for instructions like an Omnibot in ready mode. The image came naturally; we'd graffiti'd an Omnibot 2000 ad at a bus stop last week. The original text on the ad had read, *Tell him where to go.* Jim had changed it to, *Tell him to fuck your mom.* Not the most subtle work, but on-par for Anarchy Jim.

I heard feet on the stairs, slower than I'd have thought. Cops really were out of shape. It wasn't just a cliche. I considered sticking around just to taunt them. At vampire speeds, I could grab donuts and be back before they arrived — but this time I wasn't alone; I was part of a team. Even if I could get away, the others might not be as lucky.

Jess wasn't listening to me or the coming footsteps. She was at the building's edge, looking down. I joined her, crossing under the rooftop billboard we'd been altering when the black-and-whites came: Lynda Carter for Maybelline, emblazoned with our caption: *"Now you, too, can look like a foot."*

Once I was at her side, I saw what kept Jess from climbing down. Another cop was at the bottom, shining a big D-cell flashlight.

"Dammit," she hissed.

I scanned the rooftop. None of our crew was still up here. Punks, for all their talk of unity, are excellent at all-for-one but not always one-for-all. They'd beat it, like Anarchy Jim had. It wasn't apathy. It's just how we were.

"Where's Stacy?"

"Gone."

"Fire escape?"

"Stairs."

All three of us looked. Jess could hear the footsteps now. We weren't going that way.

"What about Roland?"

"I just saw him running past Walgreens. I don't know how he got down."

Huffing and puffing rose in the stairwell. The cop below started to climb the fire escape.

We were trapped — us up here with Lynda Carter and her homogenizing, mainstreaming makeup. Or at least that's what Jess and Watlin thought, seeing as humans didn't consider jumping from this far to be a viable option. They didn't know who I was, or what I was. Officially, I was a 17-

year-old human runaway from San Antonio. I earned cred because I'd told them that at age 10, I'd seen the Sex Pistols show in my home town that had started it all. Or, in the case of Watlin, I'd earned cred because I'd visited the Alamo.

I thought fast.

"That way!"

Pushing. Shoving. Then I turned Watlin and Jess to look into my eyes. My heart hammered. I glamour well, but it's hard under pressure.

"We took the fire escape," I told them. "There was no cop climbing up to get us."

"We took the fire escape," Jess repeated.

"Hot fudge cake," said Watlin.

"*Hold it!*" shouted the cop from the stairwell, coming around the corner, seeing us, entirely out of breath.

I pushed Jess and Watlin off the roof, jockeying mid-air to put myself beneath. We hit the concrete with my back, my arms losing rigidity on impact as my spine shattered. The hit made me drop Jess and Watlin at the last minute — just a little, just enough to rack their marbles. It'd add veracity, later, when they woke up with bruises.

My paper-thin glamour snapped. Jess blinked, looking at the fire escape I'd told their minds we were about to climb down. She seemed to be struggling to make sense of what'd happened (not only was the fire escape a good twenty feet away, but there was also a uniformed officer at the top of it), but her green eyes blinked a few extra times and made it work. She looked at me, then, writhing as my backbone took its time to knit.

The pain was intense. To distract myself, I focused on our portfolio of subvertisements, many of which were visible. Down the block was Larry Hagman advertising BVD underwear — an acronym Stacy had spelled in red paint as

Be Victims, then Die. There was a Swatch ad on which we'd spray-glued a photo of Ronald Reagan with a speech bubble: *Pay attention to TIME, not my CRIME.* Further up, an Excedrin placard: *I had a headache THIS BIG* ... and we'd slapped an ICBM between the hands of the woman who'd taken Excedrin to make it all better.

I thought, *We've hit this area too much. No wonder they found us.* We'd stayed close to UT, not diversifying enough. Boner move. Now the police had eyes on us, and might be able to nail us by sight. I'd have to catch the on-site cops to fix that, and it wasn't worth the risk. Not with Jess and Watlin here to see it, so soon after falling safely from a building.

"Are you okay?"

Jess. Whispered low, because now the cops were shining their lights downward. They were likely confused — probably thought they'd been seeing things, since suspects didn't just jump off roofs. So far, we were unseen. That would change if we didn't move.

Without the car, we'd need to do it on foot. And it was a mile or two — good thing the cops were out of shape.

"I'm okay," I told her.

Jess's face scrunched. Something was bothering her. I'd done my best to act human during my time with the punks at the squat, but every once in a while I'd had to do something vampirish — like jumping off a building, glamouring troublemakers who came to rumble, or never going out in daylight. Most of the crew rolled with it; they had other things to be apathetic about. But Jess was sharp, with some college under her belt. In some ways she was a transgressor like me. She didn't accept easily; she knew something was off. She found it strange that I claimed to be allergic to sunlight, that I acted like I did. Right now, she was wondering what had hurt me if we'd simply climbed down. One more piece of evidence that I wasn't what I seemed.

She let it go, though, in the spirit of bigger fish to fry.

"That way." I pointed through a construction site: a foundation for yet another downtown tower being poured over what used to be our favorite hauts. No more concerts at the Low Down, no more bouncers who took the worst fake IDs, no more Wall of Fame in the bathroom, ranking the very best graffiti. The whole block had been razed, including Nev's convenience store. No more coffee with hazelnut creamer for free, either. But on the bright side, once the new tower was built, we'd be able to apply for low-interest loans. Would never get them — but hey, it'd be fun to try.

We ran, dodging concrete and rebar.

We were clear of the site a diagonal block later. Watlin began to show signs of life in the form of deep, exhausted breaths. I faked fatigue, but Jess seemed barely winded. She kept looking at me, assessing something unknown. Or possibly very known indeed.

"Maurice," she said. "How exactly did we—?"

"Listen," I said.

I held up a finger, cocking my ear to the city. It was Wednesday night, far enough now from campus that the air was quiet — for human ears, anyway, though I could hear a thousand conversations behind closed doors. There was, in fact, nothing loud enough for the others to hear, but I pretended to strain to hear anyway. I was buying time again, wishing Watlin weren't here, wanting to pause long enough to do Jess's glamour right.

Finally, blessedly, there came a siren. Right on cue.

"What?" Jess asked, because the siren wasn't coming from where we'd been.

"I guess it's nothing," I said.

She gave me an extra few seconds, but then we started to walk. We neither saw nor heard cops chasing us. It was dark; we were in a questionable area where we felt at home but middle-class folks would not. I'd lost my orientation in the rush and the fear of discovery, but now I found it again. We all did — new construction notwithstanding.

Ahead were our usual haunts. Home away from home, if we'd had homes. The old laundromat, the pay phone where Hardcore Sally had given Watlin's friend a concussion, a parkside bench where we'd taken Polaroids of those winos fucking. That meant that just two blocks up was The Whiskey Dick. People talked like the scene was all about Liberty Lunch, The Vault, Hole in the Wall, maybe Duke's Royal Coach Inn or Club Foot. But for us, it was The Whiskey Dick. One-buck shots of bad bottles the owner wanted to throw away, and all the best shows on their F-tier circuits: Black Flag, Wasted Youth, Circle Jerks, Bad Brains. Rumor said that Jello Biafra was even vomited on twice there in one night. You didn't get that kind of thing when Duran Duran played the Erwin Center.

Two blocks from the squat, a posted sign told us that the wasted factory would soon be a McDonald's. But it also told us, from a distance, that at least some of our subvertisement crew had gotten away clean.

The sign had originally read:

The Fleur-de-Lis Development company presents
"Something new to downtown!"
Coming Soon:
A newly revitalized future

BELOW WHICH SOMEONE added in fresh spray paint:

We fuck goat buttholes!

"Jim was here," Jess said as she read it.

Watlin, two steps behind us, announced that he was hungry.

FOUR

UNDER THE SKIN

4am. I was wide awake after the others had gone to bed, staying close to the couch so that if anyone stirred, I could bury my face and pretend I was sleeping. One of the reasons I'd chosen to crash with punks (other than their stance against '80s materialism) was because more than the other tribes, punks were mostly nocturnal. They didn't rise at dusk or dawn; they woke around 2pm and went most of the night. Their schedule made it easy for me to be a vampire while still being social, but there were limits. I often slept when the others went out, sticking to the abandoned building in which we'd squatted. I tried to make things believable. Faking nighttime sleep was part of it.

Otherwise, I had a stack of newspapers to occupy my time. The building still got a morning delivery, and every evening I went down to retrieve it. Back in '85, scanning papers was all I could do to keep my ear to the ground, especially since my fellows' apathy made the idea of going to the library for research seem weird. With the squat dark and just a battery-powered camping lantern for light, I flipped through pages as quietly as I could.

Looking. For *something*.

I couldn't shake the feeling that there'd been more to tonight than was apparent. On the surface, it made sense that the cops had shown up to stop us, seeing as we'd hit the same neighborhood again and again. If I were a cop — and if I cared about the recent vandalism, rabble-rousing, and general anti-society meddling near 38th Street as much as a precinct captain should — I'd stake out the few-block radius, watching for shadows. A lot of our target area was dead, and went quiet at night. We'd have been easy to spot, I was sure, by any cops who were watching.

But we hadn't been spotted by watching cops. The squad cars tonight had come from the direction of the Drag, from the UT campus. They'd been summoned, not piqued.

I'd been puzzling a sense of not-quite-right ever since returning, since making sure everyone made it back to the squat alive. All had, though Anarchy Jim had tripped on a stair and bled all over the concrete. Nobody cleaned up the blood. They just fell asleep, one after the other, succumbing to booze and adrenaline come-down. I got up once the last was snoring, went into a moon-facing alcove beside a busted window, and read. I kept hoping that something somewhere would ease the prickling feeling I felt on my spine.

Something was happening. We weren't just a bunch of assholes whole been screwing around and been caught. It wasn't just tonight, even. I'd felt watched for weeks.

I sat in the moonlight and pondered. My mind tried to assemble the puzzle from a hundred scattered pieces.

The police tonight hadn't come from the front side of the billboard. They'd arrived from the rear. From the street, there was no way they could have seen what we were doing. We'd only seen them when we went to the edges and looked down. And that made me think: Maybe the cops only knew we were there because someone called them on us. But the one with the megaphone had said, *Stop your vandalism immediately!* How had he known we were vandalizing?

You're being stupid, Maurice. There's nothing to this. Nothing to see here.

I tried to believe it. Nothing *was* wrong. We'd nearly gotten nabbed; that's the only reason my senses were tingling. But I couldn't buy that explanation no matter how hard I tried. Being chased by police isn't shocking to me. I've lived through a million times worse.

There was something in the air: a bad scene, intangibly troubling in the way bad scenes are. I was sensing an ominous presence, the way my mind flares when there are vampires around. Or more correctly: not just *vampires*. No, this was the sort of mental tingle I got when blood tried to reach me: a tingle that means someone in my line is watching — spying, really. But why? The idea was ridiculous. Yet still I couldn't shake the sense that not only was the scene going bad, but that what I felt was someone I knew, or some*thing* I knew. It was vampire *deja vu*, making the short hairs on the back of my neck stand on end.

I went through a mental Rolodex, trying to narrow my unease to a specific vampire. *Who* did this feel like, if I was feeling blood ties? I couldn't come up with anyone. I didn't have roots in Austin. But then again, I hadn't had roots in New York or Chicago, either.

"You're up."

I turned. It's hard to surprise me, but I was surprised. It was Jess. I thought she'd ask about our jump from the roof, but instead she came up beside me.

"I didn't mean to scare you."

She sat. There was a camp chair in the corner, near a

hole in the half-collapsed wall with all the words spray-painted on it. The chair was almost entirely rust. I wondered if it'd hold her. It did.

"Can't sleep?" she asked me.

"I'm just ..." But we'd both looked at the newspapers. The way she'd seen me studying them, it must have looked like I was taking them serious — one more reason for Jess to look at me funny. Newspapers represented society, which represented structure, which represented the whole bullshit system we stood against. I might as well have been a kid caught looking at *Playboys*.

"It's fine," she said. I wasn't sure what that meant, but was glad for the lack of questions.

I watched her. I considered telling her I was ill-at-ease. I decided it wasn't a good idea. I was spooked for reasons unknown, but as far as the others were concerned, our caper was over. My compatriots seldom thought about the future, even as far ahead as next week. Our life went: *party, sleep, hardcore shows, drink, sleep, repeat.* I was trying to find a pattern in those newspapers — in searching my blood for vampire doings that might have my subconscious rattled — and that was just one more schema, one more system. In theory, the others stood for anarchy. Just because a strange itch had gotten under my skin, that was no reason to rock the boat. I had nothing, not even suspicion. This was unsubstantiated unrest: a sense that somewhere, a thing you don't know was lying in wait, ready to trip you.

Jess looked over my stash of newspapers, then crossed her legs. Something caught her eye, or her ear. Nothing I could see or hear — and I'm a vampire.

Jess stood. She went to the edge of the hole and looked down.

"Dammit," she said.

Now I could hear it.

Now, more than before, I could *feel* it.

I hadn't looked out the window. But still I knew we had visitors, and in my head I counted thousands of them.

FIVE

THE WORM AND NOTHING ELSE

Jess walked ahead of me holding the three-foot piece of yanked-out pipe we called The Fucker, banging it against walls as she walked past the sleeping troops. When Roland protested, she hit him in the stomach.

"Stop bitching and get up," she said. "Trouble."

I was unsure on the idea of "trouble." I'd peeked out after Jess, before she'd grabbed the pipe. All I'd seen was Drag Worm Ian, contradicting my creeping (but apparently unfounded) certainty that we were surrounded. I was willing to bet Jess felt just as conflicted. She'd reacted with worry when she'd looked through the window, and now was calling for trouble. Had she seen something I hadn't? Had there been others besides Ian, all of whom had leapt into the shadows when I'd taken the window? I still felt the sensation of hands around my throat, sure that as soon as we went outside, we'd find others I could feel but not see. It was the strangest sensation: as if my very blood were screaming. As if unseen forces were lining up for battle — and perhaps had been for a long time.

"*The fuck*, Jess," said Anarchy Jim, rousing. His leg was

bleeding through his bandage. He should really see someone about that.

Stacy Grace, with all her tattoos on display, was sitting on the edge of a cot we'd rescued from a dumpster behind the hospital. She looked at Anarchy Jim and said, "Just get up, Jim."

"Or you could come over here." He pulled back the blanket covering him on the couch. His little black mohawk was smashed sideways. He wore his signature army surplus jacket. He'd been wearing shades even while sleeping, and was now propositioning the person most likely in the group to kick his ass. Not even his ex — not that Jess, who was off-again with him right now, was prone to jealousy.

Stacy ignored Jim, standing to follow Jess. She was fully dressed. Sleep wasn't something people prepared for in advance at the squat. It just kind of hit you, like a staph infection.

Now I could hear them outside — all those aggressors I hadn't seen but could feel like ghosts. *Them*, not just Ian. I focused, counted sets of steps inside my mind. I decided there were at least a dozen people outside, coming from two directions at once. So I *hadn't* been wrong; Ian *wasn't* alone. A dozen people was far from the thousands I'd sensed moments earlier, but at least it wasn't nothing.

Now Jim seemed to hear it too, and rose. He glanced at Jess, glanced at the others, then did his pretend-I'm-in-charge thing. He held out his hand and said, "Give me the pipe."

"Piss off, Jim."

"Then get me a bat."

Neither Jess nor Stacy dignified that with a response.

Jim sighed and went to get his own bat. By the time he got back with a Louisville Slugger, we'd started down the stairs. I didn't feel quite as wary by now (my senses had confused me too much), but I did feel *something*: a magnification of the weirdness that'd been bugging me all night, a sense of something not-quite-right.

Bad scene, I told myself. *This is just another bad scene — nothing to worry about.*

The mantra didn't help. I was fit to crawl out of my skin, nowhere near my usual state of calm. I'd felt thousands, heard dozens, and seen only one man. It was the kind of vibe that makes you wonder if you might still be dreaming, or perhaps are crazy. As if the very world is conspiring against you.

I nudged my way to the front, wanting for reasons unknown to hit the door first.

Opening up, I saw Ian.

Nothing else.

"Hey guys," he said.

Nobody moved. There was something in the air.

"Can I crash with you?"

Stacy exhaled. "Why?"

"Yeah, why?" asked Roland, at the rear with his enormous red mohawk. "Go back to the Drag, dickhole."

Ian looked around in the wee-hour darkness. He seemed bothered, but I was bothered by something else. It really was just Ian out here — not thousands of aggressors, not even ten. I asked myself again: *Is someone hiding, waiting to spring?* But no, there was nowhere to hide. Our squat was an unfinished office building, four stories tall, surrounded by a lot with empty streets beyond. Nobody hiding. Nobody here.

It's all in your head, man, I heard inside. But whose voice? I suppose it was my own.

I cut away from the door, sliding sideways, letting the

others deal with Ian. I wanted to drop my itching worry, but I knew I wasn't the only one feeling it. Jess had looked out first, and her instinct had been to grab a pipe. The rest had roused and also gone for weapons. My own antennae were a mile tall, sure we were walking into a melee. Which wasn't unusual, by the way; we fought other punks and we fought the mods and we fought the bums and we sometimes fought Drag worms when they got riled and thought we had something worth stealing. Mostly we fought rednecks, sometimes skinheads, sometimes drunk assholes who got out of line after a show at the Whiskey Dick. But *this* ... ?

Strange night. High moon, almost full. I could see everything even without vampire sight, even without streetlights. It dawned on me that I'd felt disquiet for weeks, maybe longer. Something building inside, giving me a hair trigger without an apparent cause.

Around the building. Nobody home.

When I reached the front door again, Roland was shoving Ian and Stacy was yelling at Roland. I came up next to Anarchy Jim.

"I don't want him here," Jim said.

"Ian's okay," I told him.

"This is how it starts," Jim said. "You give these fucking kids an inch, they take a mile."

It was a stupid argument. The squat wasn't ours. By definition it was a place we were *squatting*. The idea that Jim would be righteous about it (and Ian's place in it) was absurd. I stared at Jim until he spoke again.

"Fine," he said. "Whatever, dude. Stay, don't stay. Like I fucking care."

We didn't have a leader, so decisions like this took consensus. There was a lot of muttering and then everyone just kind of went away. It was as close to an agreement as anything.

In the end it was only me, Jess, and Ian. Staring at each other, trying to shake the feeling that something was amiss and we just weren't recognizing it.

"Ian ..." Jess said. "Are you alone?"

"Well ... yeah." Unconcerned, unbothered by the odd air. "So I can stay?"

Jess looked at me: *You felt something, too, right?*

"I can stay," Ian announced.

He pushed past us, the body odor of weeks in a gutter hot on the breeze of his passage.

I did a final lap. I was the last one inside.

I went back to fake-sleep uneasy, sure that something — I didn't know what — was beginning.

SIX

BUNKMATES

I woke to a soft touch, nestling into bed beside me.

I startled, confused for two heartbeats. In the in-between moments that separate sleep from reality, an instinctual part of me wanted to huddle closer.

"Celeste," I muttered.

Except it wasn't Celeste. The smell betrayed that much: weeks without bathing, hygiene a foreign concept. It was Drag Worm Ian, sharing my bedsheets.

I startled, hitting my head on my closet's low ceiling.

"The fuck?"

I looked down at the newcomer. His jacket was either made of duct tape or covered entirely in it. His face was serene, nestling into blankets he'd stolen from me. The door was ajar, Ian already moveless. I could feel the heat of the sun: deadly out there, as if I were the sole survivor in the middle of a nuclear fire. Well, one of *two* survivors, anyway.

"Ian," I said.

His head turned. He didn't look entirely awake. He said, "Muh."

"*Ian!*"

"Zuh. Grmm."

I pulled one knee to my chest, kicked him like a piston. His eyes came open immediately.

"What the hell?" He stared at me. Ian had center-parted hair that was long on top, always flopping over his face so he had to peer through it like a curtain. *"Maurice?"*

"Good morning."

He yawned as if I was serious in my greeting, stretching. "Good morning."

"No, let's try again." I kicked him a second time. "GET OUT."

"Ow! What the hell?"

"You're in my bed."

"This isn't your bed."

I punctuated each word with kicks: "THIS. IS. MY. BED!"

"I thought everything is for everyone?"

"Not in here. Who the fuck just climbs into bed with someone?"

Ian tried to close his eyes. He grabbed the sheets. I kicked him again, foot-in-face this time. I probably came a centimeter from breaking his nose. If I'd been wearing boots, I would have.

"THE FUCK, MAN!"

He was up in my face. Close. Then his anger evaporated as quickly as it'd come and he was just Ian again.

I said, "What are you on?"

"Nothing."

"You're drunk. You're high."

"Maybe just a little."

"You need to get out of here. Now. This is my spot. Find your own."

He opened the door enough to look out. I could feel the

waft of solar heat like when you lower the door of an oven. I backed up into the darkest corner — not far, because the closet was tiny. I kept it closed every daytime, nobody bothering my undead sleep. What Ian had done wasn't just rude. It was downright deadly.

Feeling the sun like a ticking clock, I grabbed Ian's duct-tape collar and yanked him close. My will met his, clashing in glamoured eyes.

"You want very badly to get out of here," I told him. "You're *dying* to go sleep on the couch. Or on the floor. You're dying to go *anywhere* that's not inside this closet. Got it?"

"I'd rather sleep here, Maurice."

Shaking him, holding his eyes. But the glamour was hard. I could feel it failing to take hold. What *was* he on?

"Ian?"

"Yeah, dude?"

"*You want to sleep on the couch. You want to leave my door closed.*"

"I don't, really. Someone filled that couch with farts."

"Ian!"

"What?"

"Go! Now!"

He finally got up, but it was like doing me a favor. I heard mumbling until he settled down unseen.

With the door closed, the temperature inside my closet seemed to drop a hundred degrees. I slept fine after that — too fine, maybe. I woke to find I'd lost more than ten hours in a blink. I hadn't dreamed or woken. Hours had gone like minutes.

I opened the door slowly, finding the squat in long shadows and bright slants of waning daylight. I seemed to be alone, except for Drag Worm Ian. Ian was on the largest couch, spread out, one of the day's last sunbeams across his face. He was so sweaty, he'd turned the sheets dark. He was sleeping fitfully, still purging some psychedelic poison from his system.

I walked barefoot to the kitchen, where our super-long power cord to the building next door ended in a coffeemaker.

My head woke slowly, but the feeling of lost hours still dogged me. I had the feeling I sometimes get after I nap: that I've woken out of place and time. I went through the ritual of making coffee, letting it center me. I poured and drank. The caffeine wouldn't affect me much, but calm came from the doing.

I stood with the cup to my lips, looking across the room and out at the last deadly daylight.

Unsettled. Some disturbed feeling in my gut.

It wasn't just Drag Worm Ian's arrival that bothered me, though last night's weirdness hadn't helped my nerves. Ian was a nomad; he'd always come and gone. When he woke, we'd kick him back to Guadelupe and go on with our lives. With Ian around, I felt like a cause was begging to be honored: "Help the homeless," maybe, even though we all knew Ian had a home if he wanted it. The idea jarred my bones. In those years, the last thing I wanted was a cause — unless it was the cause of "messing up all the other causes." The world was fucked; everyone was out for themselves; America and Russia were always wagging missiles at each other despite Gorbachov, despite Glasnost, despite the official version of things. We had hostages in the middle east; we'd seen bankers defrauding clients. There wasn't a lot to believe in — and given my separation from Celeste, I didn't have my usual home to come back to. It was the age of excess, but also the age of nihilism. I could have chosen to believe in anything, but it was so much easier to believe in nothing.

I thought this while standing in our bathroom where the plumbing didn't work, where the walls were unfinished concrete and the toilet was a hole in the ground. Sometimes people shit in it when they were drunk, but common courtesy asked shitters to go to the lot's corner, to the spot nearest the new bank construction, and take dumps under the lean-to made by lumber and corrugated sheeting. The squat's bathroom was more for privacy, and changing, and washing up in a bucket of water we replaced whenever we got around to it. There was hair dye in there, and hairspray, and an open dozen of grocery store eggs that were slowly going bad — for egg whites, for ambitious hairstyles like spikes and mohawks. Roland sometimes used Elmer's glue in his. Roland's mohawk was heroic, but I often wondered how he slept with the huge thing on his head.

I looked myself over in the cracked mirror. I fussed with my hair, trying to spike it, then on impulse grabbed a bottle full of blue dye and did what was easy. More ended up on my forehead and hands than my hair. Really, I should give it up. Be like Watlin. Be content to join the counterculture, but not look like it at all. I could fake punk if I had to, but I always felt like a poseur.

I came out to find Anarchy Jim back from wherever they'd all been, sitting deep in a dumpster-rescued armchair. Drag Worm Ian was snoring across from him.

"You just getting up, dude?" Jim asked when he saw me.

I sat. "Yeah."

"That's cool."

"Are we the only ones here?"

"We're the only ones here, dude."

"Where did everyone go?"

Jim shrugged. "Who knows? I'm not captain of this ship."

"Where did *you* go?"

"Me and Jess went to see *The Breakfast Club*."

"Not *Rocky IV*?"

"Nah, man. She tried. I told her it was propaganda. She said it was just a good time. But that's how things get their power, y'know? People think they're just going to see a movie, like chilling out and relaxing, just watching a screen, whatever, that's cool. But do you know who Rocky fights, man? He fights a *Russian*. Just like in the new *Rambo*? Fights a *Russian*, dude. But everyone just cheers and eats their popcorn, and meanwhile it's just programming, like programming your mind to be a good American."

"I thought Rambo went back to Vietnam in the new movie."

"Yeah dude. And do you know who's really in charge the whole time? *Russians*. Propaganda. *Government*. Us and the Russians? We're just people. It's governments that fuck it up."

Jim looked over at Ian. I guess his tirade had ended.

"What's he still doing here?" he asked.

"He spent the day."

"Well, he fucking stinks, dude. Did Jake the Suit tell you about that lady?"

Having a conversation with Anarchy Jim was like watching a tennis match between two terrible players. Sometimes you could follow a simple volley as it went back and forth, but more often than not you had to track down conversational shanks that went wildly off course, shooting into the stands.

"Jake was here?" Too bad. I liked Jake. He was a mod, but punks could get along with mods if they wanted to.

"Yeah. He said he wanted to tell you about some lady."

"What lady?"

"*This* lady, dude," Jim said.

He handed me a small white card. I looked at it. It read: *Leigh Everness, Executive Vice President, Fleur-de-Lis Development.* Below that was a phone number.

"Fleur-de-Lis?"

"Yeah. They're the ones who keep bulldozing downtown in order to build—"

I raised a hand. "I know what Fleur-de-Lis is. I don't understand who this woman is or what she wants from me."

"I don't know. But she asked for you by name."

"By name?"

Jim nodded. "First and last."

Fleur-de-*fucking*-Lis. I shook my head, wanting to swear. They must have figured out we were behind the subvertisements happening in the neighborhoods they were gentrifying — or at least that I was. They'd probably called the cops on us last night. Maybe they'd been in the shadows when Ian showed up, watching us scramble. It was a stretch, but my mind kept wanting to stitch all our disquiet together and bundle it in a neat little package.

"She's crazy if she thinks I'm going to just pick up a phone and call her," I said.

Anarchy Jim put his black boots up on the wooden wire spool we used as a coffee table, leaned heroically back, and smoked his cigarette.

Dragging deep, he raised his eyebrows at me: *That's your call, dude.*

SEVEN

PROVOKED

I didn't just ignore Leigh Everness's calling card. I actually tore it up and threw it away. The act felt superstitious: just one more unfounded itch prickling my skin, begging me to obey. Now, at least, I wouldn't be tempted.

Later, back in the living room, someone tapped me on the shoulder: "We have to talk."

I looked up. It was Jess. She had an unusual look — one I found entrancing, and that's saying a lot for a vampire's sense of aesthetics and beauty. She had dark skin and raven-black hair, but her eyes were green. I think she had Irish ancestry on both sides, far in the past, and those eyes survived as recessive genes through black parents and grandparents.

I'd been looking through the broken-out southern window, past the exposed rebar in the frame. Through the window was a streetside phone booth, now under the apron of a streetlight, covered in grafitti and stickers for bands we liked. It'd become a thing: see a hardcore show, grab stickers, plaster them on the 38th Street phone booth. I suppose it was our way of staking our claim, the way dogs piss to mark territory. With Nev's coffee shop bulldozed to make way for a bank, I suppose we felt a subconscious need to claim what was still ours.

"Okay," I said.

"Not here."

"Why not?"

"Just because."

I looked around. There were others in the front rooms, chattering, playing cards and drinking. I didn't know them all. People came and went at the squat, with just a core crew (me, Jess, Anarchy Jim, Stacy, Roland, and Watlin) as constants. Right now I could see lots of wildcards: a few mods led by Jake the Suit in his quasi-formal black-and-white, a few punks from different tribes including *faux* twins Ginger and Danno, plus two big guys dressed in black who I'd seen before but whose names I didn't know. The last didn't belong to any tribe, but were always welcome because they brought beer and were crazier than everyone else.

"I need to stay here," I told Jess.

"Why?"

"I need to make a phone call." One problem with being a vampire is that it's hard to forget. I'd destroyed Leigh Everness's card, but of course I still recalled everything on it. I'd been staring at the phone booth for most of the evening, wishing my mind was blank so calling wouldn't be an option. I'd moved in with punks to be isolated inside a group — to forget the past for a bit, to cut myself off. This thing with Fleur-de-Lis couldn't possibly tie to my world, but somehow I still felt that calling the number on that card would make loose ends in my life, not cut them away.

"Let's just go for a walk."

"What's this about, Jess?"

"It's about last night. About something I've been feeling. Something that's been bugging me."

That appealed to me, but how could Jess possibly have the kind of answers I needed? It felt like more loose ends, not fewer.

"I'll pass," I said.

But Jess wasn't good at taking no for an answer.

"Come on." She extended a hand. I stared at the hand, then her face.

"Give me a hint," I said.

"How did we get down from the roof last night?"

"We climbed the ladder."

"You'd think I'd remember climbing down a rooftop fire escape," she said. "But I don't."

"I guess you were drunk."

"I don't drink."

"I don't know what to tell you, Jess."

"You took quite the punishment when those three rednecks showed up last Tuesday," she said.

"Sure."

"One of them hit you with a whiskey bottle. You were bleeding so much, you looked like you'd gone through a shower."

"Yeah, well, I got him better than he got me."

"Healed up really nice," she said, craning her neck to eye my scalp.

"I guess."

"Did you go to the hospital?"

"I actually used superglue. It was a clean cut."

"Can I see the scar?"

My hand went to my head. Because of course that hit — and the hit Jess *hadn't* seen, when Hardcore Sally cracked

my skull open with a bat in a case of mistaken identity —
had left no scar.

"I really need to make a phone call," I said.

"Oh yeah? Who are you gonna call? Your mom?"

I didn't answer right away. Officially, as far as the tribe
knew, I was a kid who'd dropped out and left home. Sometimes I got on the pay phone to "call my mother." In reality I
was calling Celeste, trying to keep that bridge from burning.
Jess saw right through me. She mentioned that I always
seemed calmer after talking to my "mom." She'd also asked
about my wedding ring, which I promptly took off and
began wearing on a necklace.

"It's personal."

She put her hands on her hips. She exhaled, looking
away. When she spoke next, the subject had changed.

"I need to run to campus."

"Why?"

"I left my watch in the library."

"Since when do you hang out at the UT library?"

"Just because everyone here says they want anarchy,
that's no reason not to plan for the future," she said.

I waited.

"Walk with me?" she asked.

Uh-huh. There it was.

"Ha ha."

"I'm serious, Maurice. I don't want to walk that way
alone."

"Ask Jim to go with you."

"You know how Jim feels about college. He'll be insufferable if he knows I'm hanging out there."

This felt like a stalemate. I was pretty sure I knew what
kinds of things Jess wanted to talk about, with her questions
about getting down from the roof, taking damage and

healing quickly, and even "calling my mom." It wasn't a conversation I wanted to have. I'd built myself a neat little nest in this place with these people, and for months nothing had rocked the boat. Now, I felt waves. Part of me hoped I could simply look the other direction and wait for them to go away.

"Maybe I'll go by the building from last night," Jess said. "See if I can remember how we got down from the roof. Maybe I can find signs of where we—"

I sighed. "Fine. I'll go with you."

Jess smiled a little, then made the smile go away. I grabbed my jacket.

We headed down 38th Street, Jess already steering us in an unexpected direction.

"Why not go this way?" I asked, leading the other way.

"Let's go up to Guadelupe."

"Down the Drag?"

"Yeah." Her next part sounded natural, but felt improvised. "I don't really like having Ian with us. He's acting weird. Maybe we'll run into some of the other Drag Worms that know him. Get them to call him back or something."

"Uh-huh."

"I'm serious, Maurice."

We went into the dark and quiet as I tried to steer us toward safe streets. The area wasn't treacherous as long as you kept your eyes open and stayed aware. Still, we could have done better. She knew best practices, yet was leading us away from them.

"I know a shortcut," she said.

And another shortcut. And another. We took the worst path toward campus. With Jess in the lead we hit every alleyway, every dark corridor.

We were halfway down an alley between shoddy

multi-unit houses when we heard something behind us. My hearing registered it immediately: three people, humans by the smell. Even before turning, I knew what we'd see.

"Finally," Jess said.

Three young men were coming at us. They were clean and well-kempt — the kind of college boys who'd tip their hats in the daylight, but grew bristles when drunk. From fifty feet away, I could smell the beer on their breath. I could see the plaid shirts, the belt buckles: wardrobe choices that meshed poorly with punks.

"Let's go back the other way," I said, dragging Jess in a circle.

"Why?"

There were two more of them behind us. Pretty by sight, but radiating menace.

"Stay calm," I said.

"I'm calm."

Of course she was. She'd steered us into this. Why, I had no idea.

"We'll just walk past them."

"It's okay, Maurice. I know you're good in a fight."

"There's not going to be a fight."

"It's okay. I trust you."

My eyes went from Jess to the rednecks. We moved to the alley's right side. Instead of moving left to let us pass, the two before us split the distance, covering the span.

"You got the time?" one of the college boys asked.

"Sorry," I said, showing them my empty wrist.

"We're late for a show. Can't find it. Where do they have concerts around here?"

"Depends on the concert."

The others were closer behind us.

"Jerry Jeff Walker," said the one who hadn't spoken. He turned to his buddy. "I don't think he's a Jerry fan, Tommy."

Tommy looked me over. Then to the other, he said, "Probably not. Probably thinks Jerry Jeff is for faggots."

I raised my hands. "Actually, I've heard him. I like him."

"Really. Is that why you've got a patch on you that says, 'Fuck America'?"

Dammit. I'd forgotten about that patch. That and my Bad Religion patch. Given number of times some evangelical stopped me to ask which religion is the bad one, I should really have ripped both off just to avoid the conversation.

"Look," I said. "We don't want trouble."

The others had stopped behind us.

"'Course," said the one called Tommy. "Don't let us hold you up."

Tommy's friend laughed in a decidedly non-friendly way, then took a half-step backward. There was no more room to pass them than there had been before.

"Okay," I said. "Thanks."

Moving toward the gap, taking Jess with me. I looked at them; they looked at us. Finally the gap opened and we began to squeeze by.

"Jerry Jeff *is* for faggots, though," said Jess.

"What'd you say?"

"I mean, *you* guys all fuck each other, right?"

All my attention was required on the five guys about to beat our asses, but I couldn't stop staring at Jess. She met my gaze and said, "They must. Right?"

Non-Tommy took Jess by the sleeve and said, "What'd you say, nigger?"

Jess shrugged, ignoring the grab, as if she wasn't sure. "Something about your mother?"

He slammed Jess against the wall. The rest of it happened very fast.

I grabbed the arm of the one holding Jess. In the same moment, Tommy grabbed me. He tried to shove me back, but I had claws in his buddy, holding firm. I pivoted as he pushed, and Tommy's momentum threw him to the ground. Jess, about to get a face full of fist, laughed. That lit up the three others behind us.

Slurs and insults flew. They came at us while they shouted, piling on in the grabby way of real fights. I had space for a while — a second or two, maybe — and used it to slip beneath their arms. A guy from behind collided with Tommy's buddy, who was suddenly no longer holding Jess, who was free, who I'd had the time to shove into a pile of garbage bags while fending off blows.

One of the good old boys had grabbed a piece of lumber from somewhere and was swinging it. I grabbed the other end, turned it around, cracked his face with it. I don't even know how the rest of the fight proceeded. I just reacted, faster than even the five of them could manage together. It couldn't have been ten seconds later that they were slumped around us and I was over them, breathing heavy, blood on both sets of knuckles.

I looked at Jess. She should have been shocked, as fast as I'd moved. As deftly as I'd handled them. About the fact, I now realized, that my fangs had descended and that, judging by the wetness on my lower lip, I'd bitten at least one of them in my fugue to break free.

But Jess wasn't shocked.

She stood and brushed herself off.

"*Now*, Maurice," she said to me, "we can finally talk for real."

EIGHT
DISCOVERED

Annabel looked at her patient. She looked at her watch. Almost an hour had already passed in their session, and from the sound of things, Maurice had just begun.

"Jess didn't run away?" Annabel asked.

"No. She took my hand. Not to steady herself, but to steady me."

"With all those dead people just laying around you?"

"I didn't kill them," Maurice said. "I didn't even hurt them much. It was just a fight. What kind of a man do you think I am?"

Annabel decided not to answer that. "You sound as if you think Jess provoked them on purpose."

"Oh, she definitely did it on purpose."

"Why?"

"To force me to respond. Five against one? I wasn't going to get out of that by fighting like a human."

"You think she did it to force you to reveal that you're a vampire?"

"She already knew I was a vampire. She just needed me to prove it."

Annabel waited, on pins and needles.

"When she was fifteen," Maurice went on, "Jess's mother became a vampire. She never knew the maker — just another deadbeat vampire dad ... or mom, perhaps. For a year, their family kept the secret. Jess never knew her father. Her mom raised Jess and two brothers alone. I don't know the how or why of her turning, but I do know what came next. Jess told me that she and her brothers kept their mother inside, helped her get a new job on the night shift, and helped her 'date' — Jess's term for luring men in as food. It didn't last long. Just a year later, she was staked. At least, that's what Jess assumes happened. She came home to find a wooden stake in her mom's bedroom, ash all around, her mother missing. Just like that, she was an orphan. Her brothers were older and could go off and get jobs, but Jess wouldn't let them support her. She tried to get a job on her own, but ... well, you know. She was too proud to ask for help. That's how she ended up on the street. It's how, years later, she ended up in that squat on 38th as Anarchy Jim's on-again, off-again girlfriend. Who, by the way, refused to let Jim defend or help her, either."

"Sounds like she let *you* defend her," Annabel said.

"From a problem she caused, just to see my reaction. Our group didn't traffic in weak women. Stacy Grace was even harder than Jess. Guys tried to mess with her all the time, but she knew some martial art. A good one. She could break arms, and did."

"But if Jess knew all along that you were a vampire ..."

"I don't think she was sure. I think she suspected. The biggest hurdle is knowing we exist, and after that it's really just following clues. Jess knew she had gaps in her memory when she was around me, that I was freakishly good in a fight, and that I healed very fast. She knew I never went out in sunlight. She'd told me before that I seemed much older than my years — a *lot* older, as if I were over a hundred."

Annabel nodded. She'd noticed that, too. Maurice looked like a teenager, but he had depth that betrayed a man much older, who'd seen more than any kid ever saw.

"I sort of knew she knew," Maurice went on. "My glamours never really worked on her. They did a little, but glamouring is sort of like hypnosis: On some level, a person has to be willing to believe what I tell them. I *can* force people to believe things they normally wouldn't, but it's not usually necessary to push that hard. Humans aren't inclined to believe in supernatural beings. They're always eager to find normal ways to explain even the craziest events. Besides, Jess was extremely logical. I think some part of her brain was always collecting evidence that I was too sloppy to glamour away, putting together a picture of the negative space between lies. Given her background, I imagine my clues were hard *not* to follow."

"What did she say, when you confirmed it?"

"My actions had already confirmed it. Afterward, it was just assumed. She said the word, I agreed, and sometime later she told me about her mother. That helped me understand her reaction when Ian had shown up, at least: as a vampire's daughter, she'd learned to sense oddity the way we do. The incident was still a question mark for both of us (why we'd been sure there'd been menace when in reality there'd just been Ian), but it was a quandary for another day.

"With my big secret out, there was no need to keep the smaller ones, so I gave her the rest: my age, some of my history, the story of my temporarily-estranged wife. She asked if I'd ever fed on anyone in our group. I told her no, that it was a line I'd promised myself not to cross. I knew vampires who shacked up with prey, but to me that always felt like keeping a slave. Just hearing it seemed to calm the last of her nerves. I was already Maurice to her. Afterward, I also became safe."

He stopped there, and for a moment the conversation seemed to dangle. Annabel tapped her pen to her pad, trying to choose a path. Maurice had begun this story with unknown purpose, so Annabel wasn't sure where to steer him. Was this about his marriage and how Celeste eventually took him back after a hiatus? Was it about selfishness — about how me-first Maurice spent the "me" decade of the '80s? Was it about his penchant for not-fitting-in, about rebellion, or about something else?

As if he was sitting right beside her, Annabel seemed to hear her husband's voice in her ear: *Ask him about the woman who came looking. Ask him about Leigh Everness.* Her mind was used to the voice by now, translating its lisp into crisp, understandable S-sounds.

Without thinking, Annabel said, "Did you end up going to see the woman on the business card Jim gave you? Leigh?"

Maurice blinked, a little off kilter.

And then he said:

NINE
BREAK-IN

Fleur-de-Lis Development had a curious office. It was in a two-story building, on the lower tier of a structure whose second floor was at street level. You had to go via a down staircase on the building's front, then enter one of several anonymous doors along a recessed hallway. It wasn't what I'd expected at all. It was too humble, too underfunded to be causing so many problems. But this was it, all right: the registered address of the party who owned Leigh Everness's phone number. It hadn't been listed in the white pages. We only knew because Roland had a friend at the phone company. An unlisted address, an unmarked place of business — a strange vantage, I thought, from which to terraform a city.

"You know, dude," Anarchy Jim said as we descended the stairway well after business hours, "this comes suspiciously close to breaking the law."

"It *is* breaking the law," said Stacy Grace.

"I meant the *moral* law. You know what I'm sayin'?"

I looked at him, saying nothing. In my rather long life, I've broken the law of nations past and present, plus many moral laws. Jess and I had talked, though, and breaking laws of any kind seemed the least of evils. Freed from the need to keep my true nature from Jess, I'd finally been able unpack the secrets I'd kept hidden inside. We talked about our strange intuition, which she said reminded her of her mother's blood hunches — a phenomenon similar to (but less detailed than) the psychic nature of blood ties. She warned me not to ignore them. I knew that far better than she ever could, but her personal experience pushed me the rest of the way. In the days before her mother's murder, Jess's mom had sensed storm clouds gathering. She'd become afraid and agitated, but her children told her she was just paranoid. In the end, the blood hunches had been right.

You feel like something is conspiring against you, Jess had told me the night before, *and the appearance of this Leigh woman feels like it's related. Don't ignore it, Maurice. We have to do something.*

As far as punks went, Jess was proactive. I'd gotten used to lazing around like Jim and Roland, but Jess was saying things I'd been thinking — that I already knew I needed to do.

But don't just call her, if you think she's part of the prob-lem, Jess suggested. *Pay her a surprise visit instead.*

The fact that Fleur-de-Lis didn't have a published address only made Jess more sure her idea was right. *What are they hiding?* she asked. She'd done the research; she'd gotten Roland to nudge his buddy. And now here we were, ready to find out what Fleur-de-Lis wanted from me via the literal back door.

To Jim's rhetorical question about the moral law, Jess said, "Shh. *Quiet,* Jim."

"You know," Jim said anyway, "it's supposed to be about

anarchy. We're supposed to be *against* the system, not enforcers of a *new* system."

Watlin threw a Totino's Pizza Roll into his mouth, plucked from a baggie he'd been rustling the entire trip here. They weren't even hot. He'd just left them in the sun to thaw from frozen.

"Jim," said Roland, "we're just fucking with their office. I don't think that makes us 'the man.'"

I almost corrected him. We were here to snoop, not pull a prank. But Jim and the others couldn't know the whole truth because they didn't know my secret, and Jim had seen me and Jess conspiring, and so we'd had to punt. I'd told the others this was light-hearted sabotage against the city's oppressor. It was they who'd come up with the idea of filling the office with expanding foam, and insisted on coming-with.

The issue seemed to settle. The office park was silent. We were well past midnight, and nobody at Fleur-de-Lis was burning the midnight oil. I wanted quiet, from our group, out of superstition. The fact that we were "doing something instead of just sitting around" (Jess's words) quieted the screaming inside my head — just not all the way. I still felt watched. I still felt like, despite the desolation, unseen villains awaited around every corner.

"You doing okay?" Jess whispered.

"I'm fine."

"You should help Stacy pick the lock. She's not ... *talented* enough."

I took Jess's meaning. I pushed to the line's front. Nobody'd grabbed the flashlight for reasons unknown and it was dark down here, so Stacy jumped when I nudged her aside. Everyone was trying their best to be quiet, whispering — except for Anarchy Jim, who seemed to think he was at the front of a classroom. The air was ominous, the streets too quiet. Fleur-de-Lis's office wasn't what we'd expected, and that left the others as disoriented as I was. Stacy had a knack for charming doormen, and we'd assumed a doorman-building was where we were headed. This shithole wasn't much better than our squat, and totally missable. The only proof we had that we were at the right spot was a hand-written sign beneath the mail slot to the right of the door. It said, "*Contractor invoice drops - Fleur-de-Lis.*"

Something dinged. The mood was sufficiently unnerving that several people jumped, but it was only Ginger and Danno, arriving in the elevator. Even the lift was ancient: something probably required by the ADA for handicapped visitors, then never considered again.

Ginger and Danno — the non-twin "twins" who'd taken the lift while the rest took the stairs — each had a barrel of sloshing liquid on a dolly. Like most of our best stuff, the barrels had been boosted from a construction site down by Zilker Park. A guy who'd since vanished, named Carl Casper, had thought they looked "interesting." I ran to UT, did some research, and discovered that Carl's "interesting" barrels of liquid were actually an industrial sealant. You mix two ingredients and step back while they expand into a very large, very stiff brick of foam. We'd tried it on Watlin before coming here: let him bed down for a nap in one of the back rooms, then sprayed the combination on him to seal him inside. It'd taken an axe to free him. Luckily Stacy had been there. It'd been her idea to leave him an air hole.

Ginger's barrel wobbled. It almost spilled. If it had, and if it'd knocked Danno's barrel over on the way down, we'd have been encased up to our ankles in foam. Mission aborted in the most embarrassing way — and unnecessarily so, seeing as the foam was the decoy mission. Jess and I, who meant to spy on what we could find, were the only two who knew the real one.

"Look out," I said, edging up to Stacy, moving toward the lock.

"I got it."

"Just let me try."

"I got it, Maurice!"

My nerves. I'm not usually so agitated. I said, "Fine. Then fucking do it already."

Stacy's hands shook as she manipulated the tiny tools. She dropped one of them and couldn't find it. My eyes saw it easily, and I used my foot to nudge it closer.

"Fine," she said, handing me the tools. "You do it."

I put my back to them, held the lock-picking kit in my left hand, then used my right hand to pull the door out of frame. The doorknob elongated like taffy and the deadbolt, which refused to snap, broke a chunk out of the frame. I moderated my pull as best I could, but the breaking wood and rending metal still made a sound like a gunshot.

"Sorry," I said. "I slipped." I stepped back. The door, shattered, sighed open. "Guess the doorframe was rotted."

They seemed to accept that, wanting to be out of here fast. They pressed in front of me, nudging me to the rear. I noticed the way Jess ran her fingers over the frame, seeing how firm the metal and wood had so recently been.

"Come on," Jess said.

I heard rustling in the dark. People shifting places. I think one of the barrel dollies ran over someone's foot, because there was a lurch and a complaint — Jim, probably. Then there was a thump, and the flat slap of a hand.

"What the hell?" said Stacy. She sounded puzzled, frustrated, or both. I couldn't see what she was saying it about.

A voice. Roland, maybe? "What?"

Anarchy Jim seemed to think the question was for him. "You're on my foot, dude."

Watlin ate another Totino's Pizza Roll.

"Come on," said Ginger, first of the barrel-bearers. "I don't want to stand here all night."

"Watlin, is that you?" someone asked.

Watlin's voice: "Woop woop!"

They'd all pushed in front of me. All I could see were shapes. I think it was now Watlin up front, slapping his hand where the door used to be. But Watlin wasn't hitting air as he swung his hand through the doorway. If I didn't know better, I'd think he was hitting the door — which, I could clearly see, was sundered and hanging by its hinge.

"Watlin. Move."

"I ain't gotta move, bitch!"

Jim: "There's another door here, dude."

Roland: "Fuck that door!"

"Calm down, Roland," said Jess.

"Fuck that door's *mom!*"

"Easy," I said. "Let me see."

I pushed back to the front, then looked where I'd just removed the door. And yes, there was indeed a second door behind it. The new one didn't feel cheap and splintered like the one I'd just broken. This door was smooth. Solid.

I pressed my hand to it. It was metal and cold to the touch.

"There's a second door," I said.

"I already told you that, dude," said Jim.

"I don't see a lock," I said.

"Of course you can't. I can't see *shit!*"

I could see fine, but I rubbed my hand where a lock should be anyway. Who puts in a door without a knob or keyhole? How would you get in? It was either electronic or openable only from the inside. But then the inverse question arose: How would you get *out*?

"I don't feel a lock," I said. "There's nothing. Not even anything to grab."

"There has to be a lock."

But there wasn't. It was a smooth sheet of metal. It struck me as a sci-fi door from *Star Trek* — the kind that descends from above or slides out from a pocket. The kind nobody who wanted visitors would ever use at their place of business.

I knew my time was limited. We'd packed a flashlight in the job bag, and it was only a matter of time before whoever'd ended up with the bag fished it out. I had a rough idea what I was facing, even though it didn't make sense. I just had to act fast, so it wouldn't seem as impossible when I did what I needed to do.

I put my shoulder to the metal door, wedged my boots against the concrete, and pushed. The door resisted for a time, but then it buckled, popped, and broke inward like a soda can's top. There was a cacophony as the whole thing came free and hit the floor: a large rectangle of alloy popping the wood on the inside, dented in the middle, probably weighing a quarter ton. It broke the floor tile where it fell, raising dust.

"I guess it was pretty weak," I said, as if shoving down a blast door was *la-dee-dah*.

"Shit, man," said Anarchy Jim, stepping in.

"Lemme through," said Roland.

Watlin hung back, chewing. The women preceded me, looking at the felled door in the scant light and deciding, somewhere deep down, not to ask questions.

All around me, with my sensitive vampire eyes, I could see the heads of my fellows as they tried to peer through the dark. They walked with their hands out, groping in noth-ingness.

Then I looked around the room we'd entered, which I could see just fine.

There was no furniture in the office of Fleur-de-Lis Development.

No art on the walls.

No light fixtures.

Not even carpeting.

There were only a dozen or so coffins, all with their lids open.

TEN
PREY

There was a rapid flutter, like wings.

I saw Danno, who'd abandoned his barrel and dolly, reach behind himself and unshoulder a backpack. He still couldn't see. I saw him fumble for the zipper. After finding it, he moved it the wrong way before moving it the right one. His eyes stared straight ahead, mouth slightly open. He, like the rest of them, had heard the sound of flapping. His hand moved urgently to find what he sought inside.

I saw his hand emerge with a flashlight. His fingers pawed it, trying to find the switch. Before he could, something struck his hand and the flashlight hit the ground with a thin metallic slap. There was a tiny crack as the lens broke.

"Who's got the light?" Stacy asked.

"Danno," someone answered.

"I dropped it," Danno said. He was getting to his hands and knees, nowhere near where the flashlight had rolled. I moved toward it, my own heart rate increasing. Something whooshed between me and my quarry.

"Maurice," said Jess, gripping the leather of my jacket.

There was ice in her voice: a shrinking, instinctual retreat. I doubted she could see, but she'd had a vampire mother. She knew this feeling — if only secondhand.

The feeling of being prey.

The feeling of others — unknown, unseen — surrounding you.

"Back up," I said.

Whoever was behind me did. I heard Ginger complain, her barrel wobbling on its mount.

"Someone turn on the lights," said a plain voice: Watlin, serious all of a sudden.

I looked toward the ceiling. There'd been can lights above, but someone had broken each of them. There'd once been windows, too, but they'd been covered with heavy black fabric that I could see nailed to the wall around them. We should have at least had street light in here — even halfway underground, even with only a partial view of the world beyond. But, modified as it was, the place was light-tight.

I heard someone flip a switch beside the bashed-in door. Nothing, of course.

Something flashed behind me. Behind Jess. Between us and the doorway.

I thought: *It's nighttime. We're defenseless, and nobody even knows what they're facing.*

We might as well have walked into a den of lions.

"Get out," I said. "Now."

"But we didn't even—" Danno began.

"Quickly."

They must have felt my urgency because they obeyed. Compared to the office's inside, the exterior walkway seemed bright. I watched them fumble blindly toward the relative light, dumb gropes giving way to informed handholds. Several of them walked across the metal door I'd broken as it laid across the entrance. Its sounds and movement, as they stepped on it, betrayed its sturdiness: a thing no human could have opened with his hands, because this was a place no human was meant to enter.

I thought of the path we'd taken to get here, following the registrant of the business card's phone number. It was just an address for bills, which could be dropped through the slot. Nobody was supposed to come here, because it was supposed to be home.

For them. For no one else.

The sound of leather wings retreated. I stayed in the room for a few seconds longer than the others, making sure I was seeing what I was sure I saw.

Coffins.

In a light-sealed room.

I counted. Quickly. I felt my heart race, knowing that when you find a den, it's often booby trapped. The room was full of caskets, and their occupants might come running back at any moment.

Three to the left. Two in an alcove. I'd already seen four in a side room, beyond where Danno had dropped his flashlight, which still laid where it'd rolled. Ahead were two more with—

My mouth opened. My heart stopped.

There were eyes in the darkness behind the central coffin. Unmoving. Watching me.

Then my eyes found detail behind them, even in the dim. The vampire was just a pale oval against all the black, floating in a void. His irises fixed mine, asking an unspoken question or perhaps conveying a threat. He had hawklike features and a thin, disdaining mouth. He must have been wearing black — probably with a high collar — because I couldn't see the flesh of his neck.

I waited for him to spring. To come at us for invading his space. Possibly *en masse*, considering how many coffins stood guard. But no ... he remained where he was. And he was alone.

Nobody was seeing this but me.

I lifted my chin just a little: a subtle gesture of advancing, as if I might come forward. In response, the still, pale face of the vampire looked at the humans now safely out the door.

Then he looked at me again.

Advanced a step.

I grabbed the rearmost human — Ginger — and pushed her ahead of me as I shoved my way through the door.

"I said, '*Let's go.*'"

"But we didn't use the foam! We didn't pull our prank!"

Stacy had Ginger by the other arm. "Fuck the foam. Fuck this whole scene."

We were up the stairs and into the quiet, singly-lit parking lot. I counted fellows, saw we were all still here: me plus Ginger, Danno, Anarchy Jim, Roland, Stacy Grace, Watlin, and Jess. One vampire and seven meals.

I couldn't resist looking back. The door to Fleur-de-Lis was still open because it could no longer be closed. I'd yanked the wooden door from its lock, then put the metal security door on the floor. From where we stood — quiet, the aural cityscape filled with distant traffic and a chorus of crickets — I thought I could see that face watching us, waiting to see what we'd do. Whether we'd stay, return, or wait to be taken.

In the parking lot was a single car, covered with a tarp. I

peeked: a silver Rolls Royce with a vanity license plate that said MOOLAH.

And I knew.

Now I understood the creeping feeling I'd had so often lately.

Fleur-de-Lis was a vampire front, and unless Leigh Everness searching for me was just a coincidence, it looked like they had my number.

The humans were visibly shaken, already filtering out of the parking lot even though we hadn't discussed what'd happened. They hadn't seen what I'd seen — not the coffins, not the face in the darkness. They didn't know what we were fleeing.

They only knew that their guts *told* them to flee, regardless of what followed. All except for Anarchy Jim, who was curious and a little clueless.

"Rolls fuckin' Royce," he said, finally dropping the tarp I'd peered under. "Materialist piece of shit. Who leaves a *Rolls fuckin' Royce* in a lot out *here?*"

Answer: *Someone who can afford to lose it.*

Someone who doesn't care.

Someone who, if trespassed against by vandals, would relish the chance to even the score.

I knew the style without question.

"Come on," I said to Jim, turning him toward the street.

As we left, I looked back one last time and saw those cold vampire eyes watching us go.

ELEVEN

ALPHA

Two hours later. Very late. I'd talked to six of the people in our aborted party, and after our chat they'd all forgotten we'd gone on our little trip. Jess and I still remembered our visit to Fleur-de-Lis, but the others were sure they'd all been down at Raul's since ten, injuring themselves in the pit for Bad Brains. They'd left after I'd glamoured them, and now they might be anywhere. Sometimes bands hung out after their shows, and if they did, Anarchy Jim would for-sure have shanghai'd them. He had a project we only heard about when it was convenient, where he used his VHS camcorder to interview bands who were willing or ended up trapped. The "interviews" were anything but — more like meandering conversations on film. Really Jim just wanted to rub shoulders with his favorite hardcore groups, and the camera was his excuse.

In the morning, Jim would probably wonder why he had no footage of the show itself. He'd probably decide he'd just forgotten to film it ... because in his memory, he'd definitely been there.

Drag Worm Ian stood in the living room doorway. The world outside was a dying bruise, having moved from purple to blue to the warmer colors that preceded sunrise. I jumped when I saw him. He looked like he'd eaten bad pork, then gone jogging.

"Do you have any aspirin?" he asked.

"Shit! You scared me."

"No way. Nobody sneaks up on you, Maurice."

"Well, you did." My nerves were millimeter-thin. I hadn't noticed the coming dawn until moments ago, and I'd had no idea Ian was still with us. Everyone wanted him out. He wasn't a punk; he was a bum. You'd think bums stood for anarchy and living off the land, but to us they were just another system. They begged; they spent; half of the young ones weren't even really homeless. They were just poseurs, looking to hitch a ride on any scene that would have them. And yet here he was, still in our midst.

"Everything okay?" Ian asked.

"I could ask you the same thing."

"Where did you guys go, anyway?" he asked.

"Nowhere. We've been here the whole night." A lie, and one that made my hands shake. I don't scare easily, and I intimidate even less easily. But I'd seen that den, and I'd seen that car, and I knew what it probably meant. I hadn't thought to glamour Ian, because I hadn't known the lump of blankets on the couch was him. But maybe this was going to be a problem. Maybe Ian was a loose end I needed to solve.

As if to underscore the point, Ian said, "No way. I was up for a long time earlier and nobody was here. You guys *went out.*" He tried on a grin, but it came across sickly. He poked me, grinning bigger, really fucked up on one drug or another. "You went on a *caper.* Didn't you, Maurice?"

I met Ian's eyes.

"*We didn't go out,*" I said, turning on the glamour.

"You sure?"

"And you didn't wake up. You've been sleeping all night."

"I have?"

Damn, the stupid are hard to glamour. Same for people on drugs. It's like the drug insanity gets in the way of the insanity I'm trying to instill.

"Yeah. Remember?"

His eyes finally glassed. Then he said, "Am I awake right now?"

I thought about it. "Actually, no."

"So this is like a waking dream?"

"Whatever you say."

Ian reached out, pinched my cheeks like a grandma.

"Feels so real."

"I guess it's a lucid dream."

Ian pinched again. "Rad."

He walked out, passing Jess.

"He's still here?" Jess said, turning her head to follow.

Ian laid down on the couch, re-covering himself with blankets.

"Looks that way."

She saw where she thought I'd been looking. "The sun is coming up. You need to get inside, don't you?"

"More or less. It's direct sun that'll kill me, but I get stupid tired. It's the heat. I don't know how you people handle the *heat.*"

"Mom was the same way." Jess fell into quiet reminiscence, but I wasn't confident enough to pick it up. There'd be time, later, to help her deal with the trauma I now knew she'd been through. Right now, we had more pressing concerns.

"You saw something in that room, didn't you?" she said. "It wasn't just empty. And that's why you glamoured all the others."

"You couldn't see anything?" I asked.

"I could *feel*," Jess told me.

So I told her about the coffins, visible only in almost-pure darkness. I told her about the vampire I'd seen watching us. That made her shiver.

"Why didn't he attack? We'd broken into his space."

"I don't know. Waiting for an okay, maybe."

"Is that how it works?"

"Depends on the nest. Sometimes nests are like communes, with a bunch of vampires crashing in the same place but with no real bond between them. I don't usually do nests, personally. I've almost always been solo or with ..." My hand went to my wedding ring, on its chain. "... or with just one or two others. But some nests form like a gang forms. In those, there's an alpha: someone in charge, usually ruling with an iron fist."

"Will the one you saw report back to his alpha, do you think?"

"I'm sure. But I don't think we need to worry." I didn't add: *Not yet.*

"Why not?"

"Because I'm pretty sure I know the alpha."

"You do?"

"Yeah." In my mind's eye, I saw the tarp. The Rolls Royce. I saw the license plate: *MOOLAH*. "And spontaneous vengeance isn't exactly his style."

"What *is* his style?

"*Calculated* vengeance. And you don't have to worry about yourself. Not yet."

"Why not?"

"Because when he comes, he'll come for me."

Jess said, "What makes you so sure?"

I sighed. "Because he always has."

With that, I told her the story.

TWELVE
BILLIONAIRE'S VINEGAR

I *knew*. I could smell my old rival all over that flashy car with its vanity license plate. "Moolah" wasn't a word when we last met and Rolls Royce wasn't a thing, but that didn't matter. He left a psychic footprint. Once you know what to look for, pretty much every vampire leaves unique traces.

Let's go back in time for a minute.

1789, the French Revolution erupts and Napoleon gets his first few shots at advancement. It couldn't have mattered less to me. As a vampire, we were always kind of in revolution, and although 1789 may sound like a long time ago to human ears, I was already 1800 years old by then. What felt to others like a great upheaval felt to me like just another bump in the road. These were the days before the phone and light years from the internet, so news travelled slowly. While the battles began to rage, whole sections of Europe had no clue and kept going about business as usual. I knew; with a vampire's speed, I was able to jog across the country at night to scope the scene. I didn't tell others, though. Once people started to panic, it made buying the best things so much harder.

You get bored after enough time on the planet. I'd fought in wars; I'd been shot; I'd had limbs blown off only to grow back. I had my causes: I'd done the Batman thing before Batman, taking on mysteries and punishing wrong-doers under the cover of night. I'd been a farmer, a courier, a blacksmith, a scribe, member of a king's court, an explorer, a criminal, a husband, a swinging single before the dawn of the second millennium. Things that people have never seen became so ordinary to me as to dull my senses.

Only two things still moved me: pain, and wine.

Pain came as a default. Wine, on the other hand, intrigued me without the need for horror. It was the only thing with sufficient nuance to keep me interested for my entire life. With wine, there's always something new to learn. French wine is straightforward, if obscured. But Italy! You'll never truly master Italy. It's all old men with ancient vineyards, arguing that what they make is amazing, and what the guy next door makes is shit.

To me, 1789 wasn't the year of the French Revolution so much as the year I discovered Chateau Lafite.

Two years earlier, they'd produced a Bordeaux that became legendary. At the time, it was ordinary: a 1787, still young, still a blood-crimson liquid in a corked bottle sealed in wax. I didn't know as much as I know now, and at the time the 1787 vintage wasn't special — nor, for that matter, was the Chateau itself. I bought a few bottles because why not, then stored them in my celler. My wine cellar was earthen because at the time, the earth was where I lived.

One of my best friends at the time was a fellow enthusi-ast. He, like me, abstained from general French life at first, and together we collected wine. His name was Raphael Michaud, and he was a bastard. Back then, I loved him for it. He turned up his nose at the world, like I did. He was recently made, just five years a vampire, and saw me as a mentor before he decided he no longer needed one.

We travelled together. Raphael liked to burn as we went. It was two hundred years earlier and on a different continent, but we were the punks of that day. We pulled capers, like I did all those years later, but killed two birds with one anarchist stone. Certain privileged bigwigs needed knocking down a peg? Cool. What better way to restore order in fascist France (or so we saw it) than to steal from the rich and give to the poor? So we stole, and we redistributed. Except for the wine. The rich of the day always had wine — and the wine, we kept.

It was in the midst of this that we raided a particularly affluent cellar, coming up with that spectacular 1787 Chateau Lafite. It was a find, even then. As time wore on, it became an even better find. We'd split the collection down the center, but I argued for the Chateau. I could feel its potential.

After the revolution, things settled and French society stratified. I didn't trust it. I'd learned to trust few things human. So when Raphael came to me and announced he planned to join the guard, I thought it was ridiculous — but if he wanted to crusade along with humans, who was I to argue? We lost touch after that, though I did hear rumors of his advancement. He always had hustle and moved through the ranks. From a guardsman to a captain, all the way to the emperor's side. They started calling him "Monsieur Michaud" in the inner circles, but not the way you'd call a man by his name. This was something else: his ordinary name elevated to the status of a title: a valuable right-hand at the emperor's side.

When France moved to a constitutional government, Raphael weathered the change, always in the mix but never in the center. I went to see him once — just once. Enough to see how he'd changed. He was the same hustler he'd always been, brilliant at manipulating people and events to his own fortune. Some of what he did to advance involved glamouring, but most was ordinary charm. There were a lot of vampires in the ruling parties at the time, so Raphael ingratiated himself to all sides. He was always neutral, never really in one camp or another. He made deals to lobby for what would benefit the vampires, then made contradicting deals that advanced the humans. Somehow nobody saw the slight of hand — but when I met with him, he gloried in telling me the details. "They're all so ripe for the plunder, Maurice," he told me. "Join me! And you should see their wine cellars!"

I left his company with the oddest taste in my mouth. At first I thought Raphael had changed, but then I realized he'd just fully become what he was always meant to be. When we'd been wine-scavenging and scrapping together, we'd been lowlives without means: me and Celeste by choice, Raphael because he'd been poor when turned and didn't have two Francs to rub together. I should have known he had grander tastes; most vampires do. He played along with my bottom-of-the-barrel game for as long as he could stand it, then reached for the brass ring.

I go through cycles, and by the time "Monsieur Michaud" had traded Napoleon for his nephew Napoleon III, I'd rolled with the idea of government for the people enough that I somewhat believed it. While Raphael moved up the ranks of politics, I moved up the social ladder. Celeste got our wealth from where we'd been hiding it, and together we moved into a mansion. Napoleon III was elected, then couldn't constitutionally be reelected in 1852. So he seized power in a *coup d'etat* — according to rumor, thanks to the plans of someone inside his camp. When Napoleon III named himself emperor, Michaud was just beneath the surface. People stopped seeing him, though, and stopped talking about Monsieur Michaud. I privately decided it was because Raphael meant to pull his own *coup* over the emperor, but I should have known better. He's a player and a manipulator, not one to grandstand. He wants power and wealth, but would prefer if nobody knew he had it.

He called on me, asked me to join him. We corresponded some, but in time we grew distant. Ten years passed, then fifteen. I made my life and he made his. He was minister of this, chancellor of that, developer and owner of this thing over here. By 1870, Raphael owned a substantial chunk of business in the Bordeaux region. His specialty, of course, was vineyards.

He was relentless. Shameless. When a competitor received higher honors than one of his vineyards, he'd cripple the owner. Too much popularity for a rival? One day out of the blue, their vines would burn. You couldn't follow the shell game happening in late nineteenth century French culture, but so much of it bore Michaud's fingerprints.

Then he came after me.

I'd had a bad run with the French Vampire Council, which at the time was still separate from wider Europe's Council. They'd never liked me, but I ... well, I'd been a thorn in some of the wrong people's sides. They didn't like my way of doing business and I didn't like theirs. I built several houses, moving between them, daring authorities to restrict what I chose to do and create. When they got fed up, they taxed me. At one point, tax men came down on me so hard and so completely that I thought I only had two choices: move away or reveal myself. I could glamour the tax men, kill those they sent to arrest me. But even that choice was restricted; my neighbors started to get too curious about me, rattling my gate, asking my help why the lord of the manor never came out in daylight. Rumors grew. Fear turned to aggression. It was strange until Raphael showed up one day and offered to take it all away ... if I agreed to give him my wine cellar.

I refused.

"Just the 1787 Chateau Lafite, then," he said.

I told him to fuck off. It was the principle of the thing. He said we'd raided the cellar in which we'd found that wine together, but I argued that he'd taken his share and the Lafite was part of mine. He told me he'd always wanted it and that I'd used my superior age, strength, and wiles to take it for my own. Lies. He'd capitulated fast at the time, believing the bottle to be nothing special. Time, however, had proven it to be a gem — complete with a full set of bragging rights.

When Raphael made the offer to buy my wine, he did it with a smirk — as if the troubles I'd had were just one big gambit masterminded by Michaud to get his hands on that one bottle of wine.

Which, I suspect, they were.

Let's rewind a bit.

1853, Napoleon III is emperor and the empire doesn't really know what to do. The ruling class had its way, but the everyday people saw uncertainty and fear. They'd had a few years of constitution, and then here they were again: at the mercy of a Bonaparte with a superiority complex. Raphael was riding the wave, buying or stealing everything he wanted. He accepted bribes of property and cash; he accepted wedding dowries meant for middle-class unions;

he took sexual favors as often as they were offered. When he liked what a shop sold, he bought it out. If the shopkeeper wouldn't sell, Raphael bought their competitors, gave away goods for free, and drove them into poverty — at which point, yes, they'd finally sell. He could have taken over the army, with all his drive and ambition, but to Raphael that wasn't the right way to play the game. You had to outwit your opponents — and to Raphael Michaud, the rest of the world were opponents. Life was a chess match to him, and the best players didn't bulldoze their way to checkmate.

During the tumult, the value of my legitimate property went up and down, up and down. The economy was a joke. As it was happening, Michaud got in touch again. He said he was very interested in procuring some of my wine collection — to aid me financially, of course. I told him no. I had money, and I didn't require much. He asked a few years later; I said no again.

One day I visited my out-country wine vault and found it ransacked. Burned out ... but with only my cheapest bottles smashed. The good bottles were gone, including my Lafite.

Michaud left France, sailing to the new world in the hold of a cargo ship. I think he planned to stay, but came back almost right away. At some point, he lost his collection — to thieves, maybe, though I'd assumed to breakage. It wasn't true, though; in international wine circles I began to hear rumors about French wines going up for auction in America. Some were supposedly from the private cellar of Thomas Jefferson — gone by then, but with those fine wines left as legacy. A 1787 Chateau Lafite was among them, "THJ" etched into the glass. I knew it couldn't be my bottle, because while Jefferson had been collecting his wines, the Lafite in question had been in my possession. But the rumor persisted and when I finally saw the bottle again, I saw that it was the same: red paint scuffed across the heavy bottom where I'd accidentally dragged it over one of Celeste's paintings. Yet it'd had those initials on it, too. I knew that Raphael must have stolen my wine, taken it to America with him, then forged the Jefferson connection. Why? Status, I suppose. A similar bottle, also with the THJ initials, sold at auction later for $160,000. My theory is that when Raphael couldn't find a real Jefferson bottle of 1787 Lafite, he invented his own to match.

When Michaud returned to France, the first thing I did was to break into his lair, burrowing through the Earth with my bare hands to reach his otherwise-inaccessible wine cellar through the most direct method possible. He'd made it easy. He was always fussy, OCD and totally arachnophobic — so instead of making wine cellars, he made wine *vaults* above ground. I went down, then back up. Not even worth a sweat.

What's more, I knew that even with so much of his own wine sold, he was too much of a snob to get out of the "billionaire's vinegar" game altogether. In social circles, we'd started to hear new things about Michaud: he was a statesman; he was pioneering new businesses that, I was sure, he'd taken over from pioneers in America after glamouring them into forgetfulness. Nothing was said anymore about him as a government lackey (the torch had begun to pass by then, and smart fortunes were suddenly in the private sector), and nobody talked about his wine. I have theories on that, too. Michaud was always about trophies more than the journey to earn them, so stealing someone else's wine was as good to him as hunting them down himself. He couldn't glamour everyone, so mostly he stayed low, bragging only to those fancy enough to share his passion.

The next night, I heard from a man named Horatio — a human who acted as a sort of paid familiar for me, handling my affairs that could only be done while the sun was shining. Specifically, I heard from him while he was dying. Horatio's wife did a lot of preserving and canning, and their preserves cellar had been demolished — the unlikely target, it seemed, of the assailant that had left him in such bad shape. Or actually: *assailants*. Whenever a cellar was involved, Michaud recruited a partner. He didn't like dank, dark places, so he'd send someone in to handle the earthen parts, then let him through the front door. He was there to grandstand, not to touch all the bugs and germs. It was a habit he had the entire time I knew him.

When I found Horatio, he was barely breathing. He told me, "He said he'd come back."

Michaud didn't know where I lived at the time. That's why he came after Horatio, who was simple to find. See, Horatio hadn't really been dying when I found him — not in the usual sense. He'd actually been drained nearly to the point of death, then forced to drink vampire blood. He was in the midst of becoming a vampire. It takes a few days to fully turn, and for Horatio (who got a bit more pain than is usual for a turning, just to piss me off), that turning was going to be hard. There would be pain, but then the pain would end and he'd be whole and undead. Then, once he was fully vampire, Michaud would return to read his mind. Or read his *blood*, seeing as their thoughts would be close as maker and progeny.

I knew I'd have to move. Once Horatio was turned, he'd be an open book. He'd be too new to know how to hide his thoughts, and Michaud would be able to learn anything he wanted to know through their simple bond of blood ties.

Fortunately for me, Horatio already had a rather

macabre solution in mind. He was a deeply religious man, and although he loved me, he loved me like a Christian loves a sinner. He knew he would soon be a vampire, but refused to walk the earth among the damned. He only intended to keep breathing long enough to deliver his message about Michaud returning, then one more.

The second message was, "He told me to tell you that the bottle was his to begin with."

I was in the progress of rolling my eyes (I'd heard that from Michaud many times before) when Horatio stood up, held a broken wooden table leg with its point against his heart, and fell face-first to the floor. He caught fire, then blew to ash. Vampire enough, already, for a vampire death.

I waited for Michaud that night. We had wooden bullets by then, and I waited with a powder-packed dueling pistol. I could have ripped his head off, but Michaud had been born fast and had military training, and I didn't want to take chances. I figured I'd just blow him away.

While I was waiting for Michaud, he used the one piece of information he'd managed to blood-rape from Horatio's mind — the piece he'd pried from Horatio's new vampire blood before glamouring his still-human parts. He found my home. He had his henchman dig, as I'd dug. And in the morning, he had his wine back.

I let it go, willing to end the feuding between us. Michaud refused to do the same. He was suddenly back in all my social circles, doing nothing to try and find me once he'd stolen my wine. But finally he did so much look-at-me — giving tours through his newly rejuvenated wine collection, featuring that rare THJ 1787 Lafite — that my pride couldn't stand it.

I burned his house. Partly for honor, partly for Horatio. My friends chased him through fields for miles, shouting that Maurice Toussant's vengeance had come. Meanwhile, I raided his abode and took my property back.

I moved to Austria.

Two years later, a gang of locals started a melee at my local watering hole. I rushed in to stop it, too late realizing that it was a diversion. My house, when I returned, seemed undisturbed. The only thing missing was a key.

To a shed far out in the country.

Where, beneath a pile of peat, I'd buried my Chateau Lafite wrapped inside a blanket. It was gone when I went there to check.

Four years later, in Venice, Raphael pulled out the best wine in his collection to show off to a human woman. Unfortunately for him, I'd already glamoured the woman, given her a long silver chain, and showed her how to bind him in it to make him weak so she could snatch the bottle from him.

A few years later, Raphael found me to re-claim the wine.

Then I found him again, got it back.

By the 1880s, I'd tired of the chase. It was stupid. But by that time, Michaud had developed a grudge. He had the wine, which I'd let him keep, but he'd made it his mission to make my life miserable. I went back to France; he followed me around the southern reaches. I'd settle in and police would show up with a grievance, or a lawyer with a summons. Raphael himself was no longer hiding. He was big shit by then, untouchable even if I'd wanted to touch him. His many below-the-radar business ventures in six or seven different countries all bloomed at the same time and he became fabulously rich. He bought the best land, built the best house, donned the best clothes. He controlled businesspeople, town councils, the government. He was in with the French Vampire Council in a way I'd never been interested, suddenly eagerly in bed with all the people we used to sabotage and make fun of. We were in different worlds. And yet he kept coming for me, kept twisting the knife. Every photo of Raphael Michaud, then, seemed to have his prize bottle of wine in the background. He held it as a prop; it was on his mantle; it was on the counter of some store he owned. He did it to taunt me. To torture me. To show me that whatever I thought was mine was actually his.

Fast forward to the 1920s. I'm in shit with the Council. Nothing new — I always seemed to rub them the wrong way. Only this time, Michaud was head of the committee, rattling his saber. I was persona non grata. I fought for a while, but ultimately dropped out. *Fuck France*, I thought. *Too much drama.* So I came to America, where that asshole would finally leave me alone.

After that, he seemed to lose interest, or else he couldn't find me. He'd already crossed the ocean, made his powerful connections, sold some of my best wine, and gone home. America was too far for the hassle. So for decades upon decades, I heard nothing at all.

Until 1985, when he was suddenly back on my doorstep, in my neighborhood.

With a bone to pick.

THIRTEEN
BLOODBATH

By the time I finished telling the tale, it was hot in the small closet: a warm body heating the confined space, whereas normally it was just my cool one. We were cramped, Jess almost on top of me. The space was too small for two people. Too small for anything more than one person reclining to sleep.

"There's just one thing I don't understand," Jess said. "Why is he in Austin?"

"I told you. He's after me."

"But his company has been here longer than you have. If you didn't know he was here, doesn't that seem like a coincidence?"

I shrugged. Yes, it did. That was the primary thing still bothering me. I hadn't known Raphael was here despite living in the city for months, and yet Raphael, it seemed, had been here first. I'd joined him, not the other way around. Was I supposed to believe that'd just *happened*?

Jess must not have thought the issue worth chasing, because she went on immediately after my shrug. "If you really think he's 'alpha' of the group of vampires in Fleur-de-Lis ..." she began.

"... which he is."

"Then why hasn't he made a move?"

"What do you mean?"

"Well, you said he always comes after you. He hasn't."

"Sure he has. His person Leigh ..."

"... asked questions," Jess finished. "That's not exactly coming for your head."

I shrugged again. But I didn't have an answer to that, either. It bothered me. I could see the small, off-white business card inside my mind. *Leigh Everness*. I didn't know a Leigh Everness. She was new to his camp, I suppose.

We were pondering when I heard Anarchy Jim's familiar heavy tromp up the staircase. He started shouting Jess's name.

"Goddammit," Jess said, perking her head up to listen.

"He's just eager to see you."

"*Jess?*" Jim called from beyond the closet door.

"Maybe if we stay very still."

"*JESS!*"

Something was wrong. Something in his tone. Behind his boots, on the stairs, was the heavy thump of something else. Its sound was uneven, either not walking or barely.

Jess heard the shift, opened the door. I shrunk back as a white-hot beam of sunlight lanced at us, turning Jess into something glowing. Her look back at me, before she went the rest of the way through and closed the door behind her, was half apology for opening up, half regret that I'd be unable to go with her.

With the door closed, I felt safe but helpless. I knew problems when I heard them, and this was one with which I couldn't assist.

"JESS!" Anarchy Jim yelled.

"I'm here," I heard her say. Muffled now. The leak of ultraviolet from around the doorframe was minuscule, but I could still feel it prickling my skin. I pressed close anyway. Normal vampire hearing wasn't quite enough. I knew, in the way I'd known it was Raphael Michaud's fancy car under that tarp, that whatever was happening required my full attention.

Jess's voice, seeing something, suddenly full of distress: "What happened?"

"He fell." A new voice. Darkly sarcastic, perhaps deflecting one emotion for another. I didn't know who "he" was, but it was clear from context that whoever it was and whatever was going on, someone was hurt. I was willing to guess a fall wasn't to blame.

"Jesus." I heard negative awe from Jess, as if she was horrified by what she saw. "You have to take him to a hospital." After that I heard small movements that would have been inaudible to anyone else: a hand touching skin, wiping away hair, seeking the source of injury. My mind painted a picture: Jess, Anarchy Jim, and at least two others, both male. One of them was hurt enough to need a hospital, and Jess was assessing him, caring as an nurse might.

"Get some bandages," said someone — the uninjured, unknown male.

More small noises. Murmured inquiries: Jess, scoping the scene.

"*Jess!* Get some bandages!"

I heard Jess stand from a squat. I imagined her confronting the speaker. I recognized his voice now: Jake the Suit, uncharacteristically demanding. Jake was a mod, usually soft-spoken. He was everyone's buddy, travelling freely between the city's tribes, selling goodies and making friends. Hearing him shout — and try to order Jess, who everyone knew wasn't to be ordered — made my skin crawl.

I heard Jess rush away. She was moving quickly while the other two dragged their burden.

The next words came from a new direction: our blasted-out main room with all the missing windows and song lyrics spray painted on the walls, where there were several couches.

Jess, returning.

"Tell me what happened," she said.

"I told you. He fell."

"Tell me what *really* happened."

Jim now: *"He fell."* Pause. "... off the loading dock behind the Whiskey Dick."

I sucked air. The club's last owners had converted a small warehouse to include a single-truck bay at the rear — but not before excavating another five feet from the low point of the dock: part of a VIP room project that stalled when the northern owners realized that Texas wasn't an easy place to dig basements. The current owners had no interest in a VIP room but hadn't sealed the door to the dock. A fall back there would indeed be crippling, enough to break even my neck.

"He needs a doctor."

"He's fine."

"Dammit, Jake! He's bleeding all over the place!" I heard her shout. "Jim! Go down to the pay phone and call 911!"

Jim's feet, stirring, obeying his mistress right away. But then I heard a new shout — the wounded, probably. Jess said, "Wait."

"Wait what?" Jake, curiosity quelling his panic.

"Where's the wound?"

The tiny sounds of fingers in hair, on skin, riffling fabric.

"What?"

"Where's he hurt?"

Rhetorical. Judging by their overheard manner, the third man probably looked hurt all over.

A groan. Words: "Lemme up." But there was something in those words — a softening of sibilants, as if the speaker had something inside his mouth.

"Don't move, Dan."

"I said lemme up."

The sound of struggle: hands, pinning "Dan" to the couch. I heard the wounded man sit up, winning despite what sounded like life-threatening injuries, my vampire ears giving me almost enough nuance to see. I knew who they'd brought now, too, from voice and context: Daniel Germain, known among the mods as Sherlock. He was an anal, obnoxious fellow who always wore vests with his tie and hip little hat. Always correcting people. Always saying "actually" and following it with clarifying specifics.

Silence. I imagined them all staring at each other.

"Are you ... Are you okay?"

"Head hurts."

Jess: "Where?"

"I'm thirsty."

Jess again: "He probably has a concussion."

Anarchy Jim: "What happened to where his brains were showing, dude?"

Jake the Suit: "His brains were never showing, Jim."

Daniel: "I'm hungry, too."

Jim said, "We have some Goldfish crackers. You know. The snack that smiles back until you bite their heads off?"

I heard Daniel forcing his way to standing.

"Meat."

"What?"

"Did you say he *fell off the loading dock?*" This was Jess, presumably watching Daniel move with the surety I could hear, amazed that he was even able to stand.

"Or was pushed," said Anarchy Jim.

"You don't know that."

"He got into a shouting match. With that guy wearing suspenders."

"Take it to the police, Jim," said Jake the Suit.

Jess now: "Why *didn't* you call the police?"

Jim said, "Because ..." Waiting for Jess to see the obvious. Then he provided it: "Because he's *fryin'*, dude!"

Of course. Jake the Suit always had acid, and he was generous with it — especially at the Whiskey Dick, where he and the owners had a *quid pro quo* agreement. The cops had been sniffing around for the LSD pied piper just as much as they'd been looking for the billboard vandals.

"Daniel, sit down!"

But Daniel's feet kept on walking. Until quite suddenly, when he began to scream and didn't stop.

Frantic, trapped, I tried to locate him in the building. I knew they'd all gone from the main room toward the kitchen, traversing the hallway. I couldn't help anyone there if I'd wanted. The hall got a full wash of morning sun: a vampire blast furnace.

Feet, stumbling. Hitting the floor, back in the direction of the main room. The screaming had stopped; I heard Jess, Anarchy Jim, and Jake the Suit go to Daniel's side. He wouldn't sit still. It sounded like Jess and the others were trying to wrangle a very strong toddler — a comparison that was underscored when I heard either Jim or Jake try to pin him for his own good, then be thrown into the wall.

"Bring me food!" Daniel bellowed. I could picture the

others examining his scalp anew, looking for what had so recently ailed him but was now gone. I heard commotion: an increasingly agitated Daniel shaking them away. Waking up, it seemed, from the lump he'd been when they'd dragged him here.

Shouts. Stranded where I was, unhelpful and confined, I was decreasingly able to make sense of what I was hearing. When things had been moving slowly, I'd been able to guess, making my own images inside my mind. But now things were going chaotic: struggles that didn't end and involved all of them, grunts, commands, disobedient grumbles. Daniel was demanding food and water, mobile but all of a sudden unwilling to go and get them for himself. When he'd been shouting earlier, I'd thought he'd been impaled — the sound was that severe. Now he sounded healthy again, although not really "well" at all. His mumblings were a mess, all over the place. I heard talk of demons, of colors, of creatures coming to get him. Intertwined with it all were Jess, Jake, and Anarchy Jim — and now others, rushing up the concrete stairs. The whole world was a party, and I wasn't invited.

"He's fryin', I told you," said Anarchy Jim.

Angry remonstrations. Struggle. I heard at least two people grapple; I heard what had to be a lamp smash and break. With each passing second, Daniel the Mod sounded increasingly out of his mind. It had to be the LSD still in his system, doing its work. Or something else. Or something else *plus* the LSD.

"*SATAN!*" Daniel shouted.

"Goddammit, hold him down!"

New voices, a melee brewing. My heart hammered like something caged. I felt my fingernails bending backward, causing pain, raking tiny slivers from the walls of my dark prison. I'd begun this wondering but had grown agitated. There'd been an emergency, then a curiosity, and now there was a whole new kind of emergency. *I had to get out there.*

"What the actual fuck?" demanded a female voice: Stacy Grace, arriving at the top of the steps. I felt churning in my gut. The whole party was coming home now, and I couldn't shake the truth that I'd sent them away. Whatever had happened with Daniel, high or sober, injured or just psychotic, had happened at The Whiskey Dick, but I knew how these things went; it'd unspooled there from a club before and a club before that. I'd glamoured them and sent them away to hide the truth of what we'd seen at Fleur-de-Lis. In a way, this was my fault.

More commotion, answering Stacy's question. The shouts, other than Daniel's, had gone from concern to containment. Daniel was freaking out: a right bad trip. He was shouting about creatures climbing the walls, a strange presence under his skin. Whatever it was that scared him, he was taking it out on the others — and judging by sound, he was doing it handily. There were at least four against one now, more by the foot count. And still Daniel seemed to stay in control. The bodies I heard smashing the walls and furniture were others, not him.

Barely breathing, I tried to get my bearings. The morning sun was to the east, in the direction of the closet door. There were steps above me, meaning steps rising from behind me, headed up to the next floor. The steps were concrete. I could break through them, sure, but might they be structural? Who knew how sound this shitheap was? I didn't want to bring it down on all our heads.

To my right, to my left — what was out there?

A wail, this one decidedly painful. Someone was in agony — not Daniel — like their skin was being peeled from muscle. I heard a splash, like a water glass tipping. But in my undead heart I knew it wasn't water. It was another liquid, hot and steaming, spilled across our common floor.

"JESUS FUCKING CHRIST!" Stacy, maybe, though it was hard to hear through the panic.

Fuck it.

I mentally flipped a coin, deciding to go right rather than left. I wasn't sure how the sun spilled in the room I was about to enter, but by then I'd rather have died than sit by and keep listening. Someone might see me, but I was beyond caring.

I went through the wall like it was a Japanese screen. Nobody even looked as I came forth, raining drywall and splinters. The scene was too compelling.

And then I saw.

A mod I didn't know was on the ground, throat ripped open enough to show the tendons. If he was dead, he was better off. The floor was absolutely covered in blood; we'd have a stain, come nightfall. In a rough circle I saw Anarchy Jim, Jess, Roland, Ginger, Jake the Suit, two mods whose names I didn't know, and Hardcore Sally, six foot two and Samoan, holding a pipe like a grand slam slugger. In roughly the middle was Daniel, covered in the dead man's blood. It was all down his front: a kid at his first birthday party, spilling more cake than went into his mouth.

And he had fangs.

"Shit."

Roland looked at me. It was early, so his hair was down, not in its usual mohawk. He seemed very short, the edge gone from his eyes. What I saw in them instead was terror.

He said, "Maurice?"

Daniel's eyes were on me, seeing a threat. I licked my lips, feeling what I already knew: my fangs were down as well — something those who'd looked my way could see as easily as they'd seen Daniel's.

Daniel came at me. Hard. He knew what I'd come to do and wasn't planning to hesitate. Daniel, as I knew him, was pacific: a nice kid, maybe a little shy. This wasn't that same shy boy. This was the monster he'd become: a new and confused vampire, turned almost instantly and driven insane by the acid in his system.

Fortunately, he wouldn't know how to use his new abilities. New vampires always take a week or so to learn—

But no, I saw that wasn't true when I dodged and he dodged to match. Daniel was faster than he should be, not unlike how vampires on Thrill, when I'd encountered it in the 20s, had been faster than they should be. Maybe it was LSD giving him twisted lucidity, or maybe Daniel was just one of those people to whom vampirism came easy. All I know was that one confused second later he was on top of me, practically foaming, trying to take my head off by the neck.

Then others were on his back, trying to pull him away, and all I could think was *No, no, no.*

Daniel must have smelled human blood because his head perked up, nostrils flaring. He let up on me by an ounce — far more than I needed. I got a vision of him turning on someone else, either bored with me or fooled into believing I wouldn't hurt him. Vampire sympathy is different from human sympathy, though. In the heat of the moment, we think nothing of trading a life for a life.

I hit Daniel's head, turning it farther in the direction it was already turning. It was easy; his neck snapped like a branch over a knee. The sound of it was loud and several people inhaled, wincing. I got up; Daniel's sideways-headed body crawled two steps away; I moved to pin him and finish the job. Roland stepped in, stupid, probably meaning to help. It was the wrong move. With a second crack, Daniel's head straightened, his neck unbroken. He went for Roland's neck as he'd gone for mine. Roland pivoted and Daniel took him in the shoulder. There was more blood, more shouting, and together they stumbled into the main room proper.

I flexed to follow, but they were moving into the light.

It all came together. Now that I saw what they'd been facing, I made retroactive pictures of all I'd heard from the closet. Somehow, Daniel had been turned. Around the same time, he'd been injured — maybe fallen off the dock, maybe pushed, maybe nothing to do with the dock at all — badly enough that they'd carried him home. Normally it takes a few days for human blood to purge and vampire blood to take over, but drugs had changed the equation. I had to assume Daniel had woken to his second life, crazy and confused, the moment they'd arrived. I understood the screams, now — the ballet that had ended with Daniel walking through the sunbeam.

As he was now.

Roland was batting at Daniel, but he didn't need to bother. The second they hit the sun, Daniel dropped off and hit the ground. He screamed an intolerable scream, taking far longer to burn than any vampire should. He was too new; his body resisted. But then it happened, and it happened all at once, and seconds later there was a torch in the room's middle.

Daniel rose, then ran. Stacy thought quick, grabbing a blanket to dampen the flames. Daniel came at her, but instead of putting him out, she clocked him and judo-rolled him using the blanket as a net. In the seconds he'd been burning, Daniel's bones must have turned to paper because when Stacy hit him with just her small fist, his head came off and hit the floor still burning. The thing kept screaming with only the room's air, no longer connected to lungs. It was a squealing, sucking sound, burnt silent a blessed moment later.

When it stopped, they all looked at me. My nerves were still high, my fangs still descended.

Stacy yanked the blanket from the body before it could go up. Jess stepped between me and Roland, whose shoulder was bloody and whose eyes were still wild and threatened.

"Step aside, Jess," I said, meaning to glamour.

"Not this time," she told me.

FOURTEEN

INCOMPLETE

The clock ticked. Annabel waited for Maurice to go on — to explain what had happened in that blown-out squat in 1985, with a vampire in ashes and at least one kid dead on the floor. She had a 21st century mind, curious in the way a long-time watcher of crime dramas becomes curious. What did they do with the bodies, and were they able to keep the authorities from becoming involved? Something like he'd described, on Annabel's shows, would have left a red carpet's worth of evidence for the right investigators to follow. But had the police even known? So much of Maurice's story meandered — enough that Annabel's notepad was full. Yet still she hadn't yet decided where to guide him.

Maurice stood from the couch. As he did, Annabel became suddenly aware how dark the windows were behind him. It wasn't twilight anymore. Any amount of time may have passed.

"I need to use the bathroom," he announced.

"But you're a vampire."

"Vampires pee," he said. Then he walked away.

Annabel sat with that. *Vampires pee.* It made sense, she supposed, given that they sweated, that their hair grew, that their hearts still beat. You just never thought of it. Strange, to imagine the undead as slaves to their bladders.

A compulsion washed over Annabel, as out-of-the-blue as Maurice's departure. She grabbed her phone and, fingers moving as if on autopilot, sent several text messages. Her husband replied, and for a minute they discussed back and forth. Then Annabel deleted the messages. By the time Maurice returned, she didn't remember sending them at all.

He situated himself, waiting for Annabel to speak as if she were the authority and himself only the audience. After it became clear that he wouldn't resume without her, Annabel obliged.

"This story you've been telling me," she said. "What's it about?"

His brow wrinkled. "What do you mean?"

She consulted her notebook. "Well, let's see. Here's what I've got: You were on a break with your wife. You moved to Austin. You're living with a bunch of people you haven't mentioned before, so like your friends in the 20s, they must be gone now — dead maybe, or perhaps just departed — but either way they aren't affecting the present. I'm on pins and needles as to why they matter. So far I know that there are vampires in town, there's a car with a license plate that says 'MOOLAH,' and that one of the punks became a vampire, killed someone, and died in sunlight. In the middle of this is, I guess, is a guy named Raphael Something-Or-Other, who apparently likes to fight over wine. But—"

"Michaud." Maurice said it without tone, disarmed by Annabel's directness. "It's Raphael *Michaud.*"

"—but it's not really a *story*, is it? It's a collection of anecdotes with no real connection between them."

"Maybe I'm building up to something."

Annabel didn't buy it. Vampires could have neuroses just like anyone else. Vampires could evade and dodge, just like her human patients.

"Tell me about Raphael," she said. "You gave me your history with him, but not how it ties to any of the rest. Right now, I'm struggling to understand why you even brought him up."

"It was his car. 'MOOLAH.' That's what Raphael's always been about: money and power."

"I know that part. Skip to why it matters."

"Well, because—"

Annabel thought: *Push him. Push him harder.* The voice inside wasn't even her own. It had a lisp — in truth: *Puth him.*

So she interrupted Maurice, raising her pen hand.

"Couldn't *anyone* have had that license plate? You said you knew it was Raphael's car right away. But how did you know it was his? Had you seen his car before? Got a friend at the DMV, so you knew his plates?"

"It was near a den of vampires operating as a company with a French name. Raphael's a vampire, and he's French. It was a straightforward thing to assume."

"Doesn't seem straightforward to me," said Annabel.

Maurice gave a series of gestures that together said, *Whatever.* "Well, then I'm not explaining it right."

"Also, 'moolah' is an American word, if it *is* even a word. But you said you knew him in France."

"I haven't gotten to the part of the story where—"

"The plate didn't say 'Francs' or anything more international. It said 'moolah.' That's *English* slang. You act

like Raphael walked around all the time when you were
with him saying 'moolah this' and 'moolah that' — like it was
his catch phrase. But if you hadn't even seen him since—"

"Okay, *fine*."

A beat.

"'Fine'?" Annabel repeated.

"Fine. I knew he was there. Seeing the car just
confirmed it."

"You knew your old nemesis was in America?"

"Yes."

She nodded. A revelation, still unearthed, hung
between them. "I see. You seemed so surprised to locate a
den of vampires."

"That *did* surprise me."

"But you knew about Raphael."

"It doesn't matter."

"Why not?" Annabel asked.

"He was there. I was there. Who cares why?"

"It's just that you implied he'd followed you. That he'd
come for you."

"He did." But Annabel sensed an unspoken conditional
to follow — something Maurice was hiding.

"It doesn't matter to me which way it happened,"
Annabel said. "What matters is your opinion of it. The story
you're telling yourself. And, in this case, the deception
surrounding it."

"Who am I deceiving?" Maurice asked. "Not you. I
haven't even finished my story."

"I don't know. Maybe yourself?"

Annabel got a hard, long stare. It was the first time, in
the vampire's presence, that she felt afraid. After a half-
minute, Maurice laid back again and said, "You're missing
the point."

And Annabel thought, *Yes, you* would *think that.* In truth, the substance of her patients' memories didn't matter. What mattered was how they perceived what had occurred. Did childhood loneliness toughen a man or make him timid? Did abuse ruin a girl's life or catalyze growth? Objective truth was irrelevant. What mattered, to Annabel, were a patient's choice of lies.

An internal voice — not Annabel's, again — said, *Puth him. Find out what he knows. Find out ... how he did what he did.*

But she thought, *No, it's not the time. You can't force people to confront what they've been hiding. Instead, you need to play subtle, to lower their defenses, and come at it from a new angle.* If she pushed Maurice, she'd lose his trust and he'd end the session. If she let it go, on the other hand, her real questions would live to fight another day.

"All right," she said, dropping it. Her mind spun with fictional forensics, with high-glam shots of evidence coming to life. How did vampires survive in the modern world, with all their crimes? "Then tell me what happened next."

Maurice looked at Annabel, then laid back. His eyes fixed the dim room's ceiling.

"Next," he said, delighting Annabel's imagination, "came the sirens."

FIFTEEN

GRAB THAT SPLEEN

Stacy Grace ran to the window. There was no glass. She was wearing jeans rolled up at the cuffs and ripped at the knees, a midriff shirt, tattoos colorful against her skin. She leaned forward. Her top half disappeared, hanging over the street below.

"Shit."

"What?" asked Anarchy Jim. He was huffing and puffing, both from exertion and adrenaline. Everyone was shell-shocked. The room smelled like burnt hair.

"Do you hear that?"

They stopped to listen. A distraction of any type was welcome, so long as it took minds off of the blackened corpse in the sunbeam and the fresh one in the shade. I watched eyebrows lift, faces tighten in concentration. Personally, I'd already heard what they were straining for. I'd heard it since it'd started several miles farther on, three or four minutes ago. I'd hoped it was meant for someone else. With each passing second the sound grew, it seemed more likely that it wasn't.

"Sirens," said Jake the Suit.

That made all of us look at the dead guy. He was on the floor beneath the twelve-foot wall upon which we sometimes wrote song lyrics: DK, Bad Religion, Fear, X, The Misfits, more. Once, Watlin had added some Neil Diamond lyrics from "Turn On Your Heart Light." He'd been punished, the lyrics scoured with darker layers of paint.

"They could be for something else," said one of the mods I didn't know.

"We didn't do anything wrong," said Ginger.

Neither line of rationalization lasted more then three seconds. For that long, we all pretended to believe the sirens had been dispatched for a car crash, a medical emergency, or maybe a fight on campus. We told ourselves that even if the police did come to the squat, we could leave things as they were and let their inspection exonerate us. Ginger was right; nobody alive had done anything wrong. *A vampire killed the kid and sunlight killed the vampire. You understand, don't you Mr. Policeman?*

I guess nobody thought that would fly because all at once, the stillness broke and everyone was running everywhere. It wasn't just the bodies that damned us. We were also squatting in someone else's building, had committed acts of vandalism, and were replete with drugs and paraphernalia. What's more, everyone knew I was a vampire now — a tidbit that, in light of two deaths and Johnny Law on the way, had been set aside. I doubted anyone would be able to play calm when the officers arrived.

Hardcore Sally hunkered down, grabbing the dead mod under the armpits. She started to drag.

"Maurice. Help me."

But I couldn't. The sun was up, the beams long. I could dart back to my hidey-hole, but that was about it. Anywhere

Sally wanted to take the body, I'd be Kentucky Fried to follow.

Jim answered before I could. His instructions were: "Wait."

I thought this was a general instruction: *Don't move the body.* Actually, it was more specific. Sally was ten feet down the hallway even without me, mopping the floor with blood, when Jim rushed behind her with something in his hand.

It was a foot. The dead kid's foot.

"Take this," he said, handing it to her like dropped groceries.

Sally shrieked and dropped the corpse. The foot bounced away and then down the steps like a badly-made Slinky. The body stayed where it was, not pursuing its missing piece. Sally leapt back as if it were chasing her. It had even fallen in a sprinter's pose. Only: *Don't worry, Sally. He can't catch you on one stump.*

Ginger found a window, leaned out, tidily threw up. Jess was beside her, admonishing: "Don't puke there! They'll see it!" As if that was the problem. As if Sally hadn't turned the main room into abstract art. As if there wasn't a severed foot making its way down to the front door that I was pretty sure would end up forgotten. Jess was laser-focused, dealing with crisis in the precise way she always did. Somehow, she was sure telltale vomit would be our undoing. I wouldn't be the one to correct her.

The sirens were closer now. Just a few blocks away. I had to stay back from the windows but could look through them from where I was, and did. I couldn't see the cars headed our way, but I did see the empty lot around us, and beyond it I saw the street, and on the street I saw two or three pedestrians — early morning joggers, maybe — moveless and looking at the building. One must have spied our presence. I saw her point and speak to the man beside her. It meant they had a reason to look, a reason to focus on this building to which nobody usually paid attention.

Then I smelled it.

Motherfucker.

I'd gone around the central stairway to find windows without sunbeams reaching through them, temporarily leaving Crazytown to the others. By the time I returned, the scene was so much worse. Best I could tell, Roland and the other unnamed mod had tried to heft where Sally, who'd vanished, had left off. The blood all over their fronts told me they'd picked him up, but already the dead thing was on the floor again, frozen in a sidelong roll as if trying to stretch his spine. That spine was loose already, though; in fact, it seemed to be the problem. I hadn't seen Daniel attack the kid. I'd assumed he'd gone for his neck like a normal vampire. But Daniel had been tripping hard when he'd been turned, and I guess he'd taken a psychedelic trip out on his victim — perhaps fighting the devil with literal tooth and nail. He'd taken off a foot; that I already knew. How? Why? And what kind of vampire attack removed a limb? I didn't have the answers. But in addition I could now see an autopsy's worth of chest wounds as well. It looked like Daniel had opened the guy to play with his organs like a grab bag ... and this time when Roland and the mod had tried to hoist him, his ribcage had spilled gore like a shopping cart. There were organs everywhere.

"Nick! Grab that spleen!" Roland shouted.

Instead of complying, the mod apparently named Nick barfed on the spleen (if that's what it was) just like Ginger had barfed out the window. The puke, which now covered the spleen-thing, made the sack of wet flesh decidedly chunkier, smelling more like acid. Despite the unspooling crisis, my first thought was, *Well, shit. I definitely don't want to eat it* now.

Sirens came closer. My fangs were still down. It was embarrassing, showing my bloodlust in this time and place. I was preoccupied with keeping my lips over them. I felt like I was a kid in high school, trying to hide a boner. I was aware enough to know we'd never pass muster — the place reeked of hemoglobin and copper. I was hungry; last night had given no time for respite. I considered telling them all to run, that I'd handle it. If they agreed, I'd run around before the cops came, licking the walls.

Hands hit me like little bulldozers. I expected Jess, shoving me away from the others' fear (of me, in part) and toward safety. But it was Stacy — as unafraid as Jess, which didn't surprise me at all once I thought about it.

"Get out of the sun," she said.

"I'm okay." I wanted to help. Couldn't, though. I was pinned. I avoid sunlight at all costs, even if I can stick to shadow. It makes me tired and weak. Any one of them could have ended me in that moment, if they'd wanted. A shove into a sunbeam, a casual wooden stake through my heart.

"You're a vampire. Don't bullshit me, Maurice.

"I'm—" The instinct to deny was strong, but that ship had sailed. So I said, "Yeah, I am."

"Go back to your closet. We've got enough problems without—"

"I got it!" a voice interrupted. It was Roland, now beside Stacy. He was holding the escaped foot, grinning like a child who's done good.

Stacy tried to focus on me despite the tumult. She

failed. Then, making it a trifecta, she glanced at Roland's gift and vomited down my side. Seeing Stacy puke made Roland puke. I backed up, out of the line of fire.

The sirens arrived. I remembered what I'd smelled — something the others hadn't noticed.

"The building's on fire," I told them. Both were gagging with post-barf, wiping their lips.

Stacy stopped. She sniffed. Then she looked up where I'd looked, where all the people on the street were now looking. Stacy did the computation, decided where a fire could have started, and stepped over the bodies. Now that the area was clearer, I could see scorch marks above Daniel's final inflammatory resting place. When he'd burned, sparks from his passing had lit my pile of newspapers. Embers had drifted, moving like emissaries. The must have climbed the walls because somehow, the fire was above us. I could see the reflection of flames, unable to go closer. The humans went all the way to the sun-drenched window and looked up, gasping in alarm.

"*Get the fire extinguisher!*" Confusion everywhere. I don't even know who yelled it.

Rushing. Fear. Chaos. Someone shouted back that we didn't have a fire extinguisher, *of course* we didn't have a fire extinguisher. Others began screaming (at the body? At the spleen and intestines and a the spongy mass that was probably part of a lung?), others began running, and none of them had a brain in their heads. Meanwhile the sirens had gone silent on arrival. I could see flashing lights, red and blue, as they traced the windowsill from below. My gut, I saw, had been wrong. It wasn't cops — or at least, not entirely cops.

"It's just the fire department," said Anarchy Jim.

"*Just!*" That last was Jess, apparently still with some brain left. Arguably, fire trucks were worse. There was a chance we could talk police away, but not firemen. They'd insist on putting the fire out, and then cops would follow. There would be questions we couldn't answer, especially since nobody was supposed to live here.

There was a knock at the door. Five seconds later there was a harder knock, as if struck with the butt of an axe. Roland must have locked it when he'd gone after the foot, thinking he could keep newcomers out. The next thing we heard was the other end of the axe, turning our front door to splinters.

The firemen came like invaders, in full suits with respirators. Jess rushed down the stairs, met them at the door. She started making things up, pushing them back, saying anything to keep them from circling the floor to find the bloody mess. I thought they'd push past her, but then I heard her voice, still below, start to diminish. She was no longer pushing the firemen out; she was leading them to the building's other end. Her fake-panic must have been convincing because I heard them follow her: up to floor three without taking the bloodied front stairs. *Good girl.*

Meanwhile, I heard a sound from above like spraying foam. Once. Twice. Three times. Short bursts, followed by a cool, sterile odor as new gas drifted down from above.

Then there were more feet on the steps, only this time from above. It was Nick and the other mod coming down from the third floor, carrying that thing we weren't supposed to have. It was a fire extinguisher, smelling used, still exhaling CO_2. Safety first. Who knew?

"It's out," said Nick.

But he looked confused. He'd come to tell the firemen, who I guess would be expected to overlook the gore if they'd been where we stood. But the firemen were above us. I could hear them, with Jess. There was low chatter as they inspected the place the fire must have died. They kept asking questions. I could hear them wondering how the fire started, feet headed for the bad staircase to come down and see.

Roland ran up. I heard him yelling. Not exactly what innocent people do when firemen ask how they can help quench a fire.

I heard Jess's voice, finding steam: "They say the fire's out."

"We know it's out," said one of the firemen's voices. We still need to see downstairs."

I looked up and saw them push past her. She moved, got in front of them again. The rest of the punks and mods filtered up, Stacy Grace staying behind to hastily throw garbage over our bloody visitor. It looked like a random mess, but in a way it worked. The whole damn squat was a random mess, and better to see than all that blood and guts.

She looked at me and swallowed. Eyes wide. Before then, I'd never seen Stacy scared.

The group, growing from both sides, began to argue. I was still out of the way, feeling the sun's radiant intensity, knowing my only choice would soon be to retreat into my closet — and then find a way to seal the hole I'd broken through its wall.

"Maurice," Stacy said, coming toward me again. "Don't be an asshole. Go into the closet. Live to help another day."

I wanted to protest, but vampires during the day are vampires under sedation. My eyes sagged. My muscles felt like limp noodles. I couldn't stay here — in the moment, in the building, in my increasingly fragile awareness. I could barely keep my focus.

I heard arguing. I felt fear.

I managed to creep back into the closet. I managed to hang a blanket to cover the hole I'd busted in the wall.

Then my knees gave out and I hit the ground, and after that felt nothing at all.

SIXTEEN

LANDLORD

My eyes opened. It took time to find my bearings. I saw that I was in my usual closet, a blanket hung to conceal the hole. I seemed to remember coming back here, seemed to remember hanging that blanket. It was like a dream.

But beyond that bit of confusion, I could feel the air's change. Dusk. It was cooler, and the energy was different. It seemed safe to emerge, so I did.

Stacy Grace was on a plastic chair across from me.

"They didn't know what to do with you. Having one of us stand guard was the solution."

She tossed me a wooden survey stake — the kind they sell at hardware stores. I caught it, puzzled until I realized it was meant to be a vampire-killer.

"I ..." I began to say. I wasn't sure what words would finish that sentence, but it turned out I didn't need to. Stacy was already standing, not exactly doing her job as sentinel. She'd either decided that if I was going to hurt anyone, I'd have done it by now ... or perhaps that if I cared to try, a flimsy garden spike wasn't going to stop me.

"The firemen wouldn't leave," she said, as if it explained

her standing. "They wanted to search no matter what anyone said, 'just to make sure the fire was out.' But I know snooping when I see it, and these guys were snooping. Someone *sent* them."

"Because we had a fire," I said.

"The fire would have *just* started when they were called. It happened so fast, it's as if someone was watching. Waiting."

"So your theory is that someone was *spying* on us ... then called firemen to *save* us?"

"Hey. Don't ask me explain 'ordinary' behavior."

I considered. In truth, I'd wondered the same thing. Those engines had been dispatched stupidly close to the fire's onset, if I assumed it had started just after Daniel burned. Stacy said the firemen were snooping, and from what I'd seen, I sort of believed her. What would cause that: firemen sent without delay, then coming in like private eyes?

"Did they find anything?"

"I'm still a free woman, aren't I?"

"But what about all the blood?"

"Jim got belligerent. He told them we were making a film and the blood was fake."

"What about the *bodies?*"

"One was just ashes. Sally got the other one down to the incinerator. It's not working, but Roland ran out and got some charcoal. Ergo, now it is."

I sat. I put my face in my hands. "So rather than talking to them," I said, "you dragged a dead body into the basement, shoved it into the furnace, and lit it with charcoal briquettes."

"Hey. You want to be in charge? Try being awake next time. The job is done. The firemen left."

I paced the hallway, the stairway, the rooms. They'd gotten it pretty clean during my slumber.

"They left," I said.

"Hell yeah."

"And they didn't see reason for probable cause?"

"They were firemen, not cops. Firemen can't do 'probable cause.'"

"Okay. And they didn't *call* the cops?"

Stacy didn't respond to that.

"They *did* call the cops," I said, interpreting her silence.

"Yeah. But don't worry. We'd cleaned up pretty good by then. Jim took on a Texas accent when they came and basically said, 'Don't tread on me!' He told them to come back when they had a warrant."

"And?"

Again she said nothing.

"They *will* come back with a warrant," I recited.

"Not quite that bad," Stacy said. "They just wanted to look around. It's not quite at warrant level yet."

"Except that Jim said they *couldn't* look around."

"Jim's not the owner," Stacy said. Then she paused a third time. It was like we were playing fill-in-the-blanks.

"So they went to *find* the owner," I said.

Stacy nodded.

I thought: *Good luck with that.* I'd done a search before trusting the squat to sleep in, and apparently our building was an aborted development project from 1977. The bank had foreclosed when the company ran out of money, and since that time its owner had been Wells Fargo's REO division. As good as no owner at all.

I told this to Stacy, who shook her head.

"Unfortunately, that's outdated information," she said.

"How so?"

This must have been Anarchy Jim's cue to enter. He hesitated on seeing me awake, but only slightly. They'd all decided not to drag me into the sun after learning I was a vampire, so apparently I was one of the good ones.

"Maurice," he said.

"Jim."

"So you've got fangs," he said.

I shrugged.

Stacy got his attention. She said, "Tell him what you told me."

I looked from one to the other. The most curious of changes had happened since my undead secret had been revealed. Not only were they seemingly unafraid, but they were deferring to me as leader. That was new. It wasn't entirely welcome. We'd always been a tribe, not a tyranny. I hadn't left the rat race and moved in with punks to *gain* responsibility.

"You had a visitor," Jim said. "She's gone now."

"Who?"

"The landlord."

To Stacy I said, "I told you, we don't have a landlord."

Jim answered. "She gave me this." He handed me a piece of paper. It seemed to be a copy of a quitclaim deed, executed just today. The recipient was Fleur-de-Lis Development — apparent new owner of the building.

"Fleur-de-Lis *bought the building?*" That would probably make the visitor Leigh Everness. If she'd come during the day, she was human. A familiar, maybe.

"Apparently they bought the whole block, plus the block next door."

I scanned the deed. He was right; it wasn't for just one parcel. It was for several.

"How? Why?"

"I don't know. But Maurice? The visitor lady knew about the fire. The cops and firemen weren't around when she showed up, so she knew some other way. And ... well ... from the things she said, I think she even knew about the *bodies*."

I felt the ground unseat beneath me. I was suddenly sixty years back in time, Michaud's manipulations a cornerstone of my life. I could see the web I was being snared in, having played right into it. We were avoiding the law, guilty of hiding a murder and perhaps much more, able to be exonerated or defended only by the people who owned the building. And guess who that suddenly was? It was too tidy. Too much like rails laid out for us, to steer us right where someone wanted us to go.

She knew about the bodies.

Maybe, I was beginning to suspect, because someone had *sent* those bodies into our home to die. Daniel and the others had come back after dawn, but the attack would have happened overnight. Daniel had made the trip to the squat before he was too vampire to survive the sun, then turned — and gone nuts — where I'd have no choice but to kill him. I had to wonder: Was this all a setup? Vampires were suddenly everywhere, after months of being nowhere. No matter how I thought about it, I couldn't see this as chance.

"What did she want?" I asked.

"To meet you."

"But you said she left."

"Not like that. She — or someone she's with — wants a *formal* meeting."

Of course. Fucking Raphael Michaud and his fucking ceremoniousness.

"And dude?"

Jim was handing me something else.

"She said to give you this."

It was a corkscrew, etched with the Fleur-de-Lis logo.

With it was a card. Another of Leigh Everness's cards.

But this time there was a new address handwritten on the back, plus a meeting time scrawled in ink.

8:30pm. An address on 6th Street that turned out to be the Driskill Hotel.

I went alone. I knew this was about me, about Michaud. Anyone I brought with me would just be in harm's way.

I stood across 6th Street and regarded the hotel's facade. I'd heard of the place, but seldom strayed this far from campus. It was all muted brown brick and concrete the color of cream, arches and pillars and railings of stone. Four stories, excessive architecture even for the day, THE DRISKILL written beneath the peak of its central roof. I'd never been inside, but the building itself was legend. One of the last pieces of old, old Austin, supposedly haunted. The kind of place you should wear a suit to enter — maybe a top hat and cane. Exactly the kind of place I'd expect to find the man I'd hoped never to see again.

I walked past the stone porch, strewn with chairs. Beneath the overhanging second story, through the opulent doors, held for me by doormen. I wasn't dressed to enter, but nobody asked questions. *Be nice to the teenager in the antiestablishment costume,* I imagined my host telling the staff, *and there'll be a nice 5-spot in it for you.*

The lobby was mammoth, all marble and polished wood, more ornate than half the buildings I saw hundreds of years ago in old Austria or Rome. The elaborate carved-wood ceiling was two stories tall. The center of the hotel's plus-shaped floorplan was dominated by a cut-glass fixture, mostly yellow, done in a downward-facing dome. Smooth marble pillars lined the intersecting central walkways like sentinels on guard. Straight ahead was a vast mezzanine staircase leading up to the bar on the left and the next story on the right, the mid-floor landing dominated by a life-size painting of a man in black: *Colonel Jesse Driskill,* according to the plate.

The business card in my hand read:

Leigh Everness
Executive Vice President
Fleur-de-Lis Development

BELOW THAT, there was a phone number and an address along the river — the *lake,* Austin called it — in one of the newly constructed monstrosities. Fleur-de-Lis's official office, I had to assume, since we'd found their unofficial one after Leigh's last attempt to get in touch. I'd run by that official place earlier: all glass and metal, a few floors made without windows: in general a building that shouted *Look at me.* Before giving Jim the card to give to me, Leigh had drawn a line through that address and written the Driskill's.

On the back was a meeting time I hadn't arranged but was expected to honor, then a note: *8:30pm tomorrow. The bar. Don't be late.*

I arrived to find the Driskill's large, ornate bar almost empty — strange even for a weekend night. There was only one large group, in the corner past the piano, almost to the 7th Street exit. They were around a large table, half with backs to me, truly visible only once I'd traversed the dim. All those backs were wearing charcoal power suits with white shirts beneath. All men. Those who'd removed their jackets had visible suspenders. Collars buttoned high — and, when I circled around to see, boldly colored ties.

I counted seven of them. The table they'd gathered around didn't have a head, but still one man dominated the rest, *making* a head. This one alone wore a blue shirt with a white collar and cuffs, navy suspenders with an off-white stripe down the center. Red tie with blue accents, brown hair so gelled and perfect you'd think LEGO had molded it.

Raphael Michaud, back from the figurative dead.

He saw me and stood. I noted perfect charcoal slacks with a thinly striped pattern. White teeth split his lips. Not fanged — not yet. Just capped and polished and buffed, human opulence perfectly imitated.

"Maurice." Falling into my French name, his accent on full display. "It has been so long, my friend."

He came toward me, opening his arms as if for a brotherly hug. All chatter stopped. There was nobody in the place beyond the eight of us — glamoured away to give us privacy, I assumed. I looked down and saw twelve other eyes on me, waiting for my response. It was the scene in a western where the pianist stops playing ragtime and all the gunslingers wait to see who'll draw to start the brawl.

I looked at Raphael. I didn't want to hug him, but

ignoring it felt too brazen, too cliche. Nobody really did that, did they? Rebuffing was a thing of predictability and pride — the opposite of punk rock chaos. Thus rationalized, I did my halfway version of an embrace. He kissed me on both cheeks, his lips as cold as glass in winter.

"You look ..." He held me at arm's length, scanning before responding. I was in black army surplus boots, ripped jeans, band pins on a black jacket I'd worn over my Minor Threat shirt: the LP cover featuring the top of Alec MacKaye's iconic head. "... *well*," he finished.

I backed away. "What do you want?"

"To drink, of course." He gestured to an empty chair, for me to sit.

"To drink," said two of the other men in unison. Closer now, I looked at them properly. They were all dressed like Michaud, almost as if in parody — or tribute. They had the same slicked-down hair, the same white teeth, the same $300 dress shirts. I flinched a little at the last man — a hawk-faced vampire with sharp, narrow eyes who I'd last seen in the darkness of their nest.

"Who are these assholes?" I asked.

"*Tsk.* You don't even know them. This is my executive team." He made introductions. The hawk-faced man was named Adam. He must've recognized me, because when Michaud named him, he gave me a smirk.

"The person who left the card was a woman," I said.

"Yes. Leigh. She took the EVP title for herself. In Leigh's case, the promise of power was more persuasive than ... well, than the way we normally do our persuading."

"So she's human."

There was a beat. I was being too direct. I wasn't honoring this fancy little dance the way he'd wanted. I knew they were all vampires. None of them had human scent. And judging by their eyes, none of them had a soul. Still, I was taking a chance. It was the '80s, and souls were in short supply.

"Yes," he said, his face losing some of its friendliness. He pulled the chair out for me, underscoring his demand. "Leigh is human."

"Food?" I asked.

"A familiar," he answered. "A necessity of my line of work. So few people will agree to buy property at night."

All the moussed hairdos around the table nodded and mumbled their agreement. I heard "that's right" and "takes money to make money."

"You must trust her," I said, "sending her to do your dirty work instead of going yourself."

I surprised a tiny scowl out of him. He hid it immediately, smiling anew. "This is nothing new, Maurice," he said. He pronounced *this* as *zees*. "When we were partners, you always insisted on doing everything yourself. It was a weakness. Alone, a man cannot grow. Leigh has been with me a very long time. Yes, I believe I can trust her."

"How long?"

"Twenty-five years." He looked at his watch, which must have shown the date. "Almost, as it turns out, to the day."

"Pity. I guess you'll have to turn her soon."

"That is not the relationship we have."

"Twenty-five years a familiar? It's the law. You *have* to turn her if she wants it ... *my friend.*"

Michaud laughed. "Leigh does not have that ambition. I am nighttime and she is daytime. I am the brain and she is the right hand. She would be foolish to force my hand. She'd either become another vampire yes-man like these fools, or leave my employ and all she's built here."

Either the vampires around the table didn't know Michaud was insulting them or didn't care. They nodded again, made little toasts again, and recited success slogans again.

"Real estate, huh?" I looked around. The Driskill, with all its opulence, was the perfect background for the go-go life of a high-end developer. "When I last saw you, you were sucking politicians' dicks."

It was too direct a punch. Still, Michaud took it as laughable rather than cutting. He chuckled.

"Ah, Maurice. You were always so quick to criticize, yet so willing to capitalize on the opportunities I created for us. You benefited from the tax reform and the exceptions I made for us back in France. I've steered armies away from your home, assisted your kin, and turned witch hunts away from both of us. I helped chase your competitors out of town, and you multiplied your enterprises to fill the void. You say I have always chased material things, yet you have always followed behind me and picked up the scraps."

I sat. Heavily, deep in the chair. The vampires around the circle waited to see how Michaud would react, and when he reacted by sitting again and crossing his legs, they crossed their legs, too.

"Why did you call me here?"

"You are occupying my building," Michaud answered.

"It's Wells Fargo's building."

Michaud raised one arm, inspected the white cuff at the end of his blue sleeve, then adjusted the gold adornment there. "Not anymore."

"Just because you found out where I was and made an offer on the building we happen to—"

He cut me off. The vampire '80s guys nodded.

"I did not make an offer, Maurice. I bought it outright.

There was no loan, no time required to complete loan paperwork. I offered a quitclaim deal, zero contingencies, and will pursue the rest of the administration in the coming weeks to make it official. Leigh was supposed to show you the deed. I do not need a title search or title insurance, because if the chain of title isn't clean, what do I care? I am doing business all over town. Forgive me, but your shithole is hardly the largest of my concerns."

"Shithole," echoed one of the men in suspenders, nodding.

"Then why did you buy it?"

"So that you cannot."

"I don't want to buy real estate. I'm not like—"

He cut me off again. "You *fled*, Maurice, before our business was finished. You came to America. You were too good for the rest of us, *n'est-ce pas?* It was fine. I did not begrudge you your antisocial ways. I, too, owe my success to breaking from norms. So I remained where I was and every once in a while I would hear about *mon ami* abroad. I was pleased with my station and did not wish the hassle of crossing the ocean to visit. I was happy for you, Maurice. It did not matter that you stole from me."

"I didn't steal anything from you."

His calm broke in a snap. He slammed his fist on the table, and all the fancy drinks rattled. A human bartender — glamoured, by the look — peeked from a far-away table.

"*1921! Années folles!* Where did you spend them? Here, in America! You think I did not hear about your adventures in Chicago? The twenties roared just fine without you in France, my friend. I would like to be pleased. I have tried. For years, before coming here myself, I tried. There were so many indiscretions to be had. But nothing could erase the slap you laid across my face."

"What are you talking about?"

"Our agreement! The bounty you stole!"

"I didn't steal anything! I was sick of politics. Sick of the greed and the pride. All I wanted was to escape."

"*Putain! Tu me prends la tête!* And who did you take with you, with this escape?"

"Celeste."

"*Oui.* And who else?"

"I seriously have no idea what—"

"François!"

"François?"

"Do not pretend you did not lure him, Maurice. François was cornerstone to my entire organization, yet he favored you with his cold idealism. You, who did none of the work yet always came out on top. If you refuse to be 'soiled by greed' — and if you can wear this *couture* of the masses—" He gestured, angrily now, at my punk rock garb. "—without looking in the mirror and laughing in your own face? If that is your way, then why did you lure him in the first place? If you wished to escape all that your old world represented, what need in the new world would you have for a *tasse débordante?*"

I sat back. So much of this was starting, alarmingly, to make sense. 1921 was 64 years ago by the time we met in Austin. Had he been holding a grudge for 64 years — a grudge I hadn't even realized I'd provoked? I felt like I'd dodged a bullet by accident but was now staring down the barrel of the very same gun. If he really thought I'd stolen François, that would explain why his people had been stalking the squat, why we'd felt eyes on us, and why his familiar, Leigh, had been seeding word all over town. That part of it, at least, made sense. The *when* and *why-now*, on the other hand, were still up for grabs.

"If François came to America," I said, "it's news to me."

He laughed. The other '80s guys laughed with him.

"Maurice, Maurice," he said, affecting calm now that he once again held the upper hand. "So little you have changed. You are not telling me the truth. I made use of a conduit after François went missing. Procuring a conduit capable of locating blood memories of François's was not easy, but once I found one, locating François himself was. I know he landed in New York. I know he went to Chicago when you went to Chicago. The blood memories of vampires who encountered him showed the same things that those around you saw. I was able to see into Santori and his people, even after you'd slaughtered them. You can lie to me all day long, but I will not be convinced."

"I'm not lying."

A man with red suspenders lit a cigar, then took his time chuckling with power, puffing away. Heads nodded around the table. Was this a show of muscle? If so, it was a poor one. I could tell the six others with us were new — probably less than five vampire years old, lured by the vacuous indulgence the vampire life promised. I could take them all down easily, if I wanted.

"Lie, don't lie," Michaud said. "Either way, you will return him to me."

"François was almost thirty when I left," I said. "Even if I did coerce him to come with me to America — which I didn't — he'd be dead by now."

"Oh yes. He's dead and buried." Michaud nodded, then sipped his drink. "I visited his grave. Knelt atop it, if you believe that, trying to reach my mind into his casket."

"That's—"

"—crazy? Yes, *mon ami*, it is. I built many things after you left. I own a perfume line, a company that manufactures copper wire for telecommunications, two advertising agencies, and many businesses that are ... how would you say? 'Below the table.' I adjusted quite well after you stole my *tasse débordante*. But then, as things happen, certain favors paid out at 36 *Quai des Orfèvres* began to expire, and those in charge would no longer take my bribes."

"You were bribing the *police* judiciaire?"

"Do not become high and mighty with me, Maurice. You have played within the law only because it has not come to test you. It's ironic, that I with my dislike of germs I was always the one willing to sully my hands." As if in demonstration, he nudged one of the other men's glasses away from him — using a clean napkin to do it. "In my line of work in America, it is the FBI I must contend with, sometimes the FTC. With them, I have had to make paid friendships. In France, it was the *police* judiciaire. They were still heavy with corruption, but by the end of my time there it was corruption that worked against me rather than for me. I was not able to buy them after a time, and without their favor so much of my backbone collapsed. I suppose it would have crushed a lesser man, but as you know, this would not be my first opportunity to rise from the ashes. I absconded with what I could, hoping when I found my lead in the '70s that François might still live, and that I might siphon what I'd hidden out of his mind once more. Alas, he had expired. But in truth, did it matter?" Michaud leaned toward me. "Probably not, *n'est-ce pas*? Not if someone had already emptied the vault."

"*Emptied the vault*," said the man to my right. His hair looked shellacked. I realized that he looked the same as the man next to him, who looked the same as the man next to *him*. So it was all the way around the table. They were all thirty-something, male, white, probably all with cocaine straws in their pockets. There was a cookie cutter some-where, and all these men had been stamped from it.

Michaud was sitting back, fully in his element. "Tell you what, Maurice," he said. "Give me what you took from François and I will spare your friends."

"You can't kill them," I said. "I took my usual precautions. If I or anyone on my protected list inexplicably vanishes, my proxy has instructions to—"

He was waving me away, half laughing "Oh, *Maurice.* Your threats do not frighten me. I have no urge to harm your people. Or *any* people. The world has changed from when we were boys. Or from when we were scheming old men together, if you prefer. There is no need to commit crime, when what passes for legal has become so sinful." He sipped again. "I have purchased your entire block. Private security has been tailing all of you for weeks. I know where you live, where you go, what you do in your free time — not that there's anything *but* free time for you these days. I know all of your friends' histories. Your friend James, who you call Jim? He was in a hit-and-run accident two years ago, at fault. A couple died, and if caught, James could stand trial for vehicular homicide. Stacy and Jessica both ran away from home, both from abusive father figures. Stacy was once a prostitute, did you know that? Jessica did better for herself, but she still ran away from several large loans — student loans officially, though they were borrowed from unsavory sources once typical lenders turned her down. I do not have to lower myself to murder to cause them trouble. All I have to do, really, is file the paperwork to evict them. Society will take care of the rest."

I saw where he was going. He didn't need to subvert the law — not anymore. Buying the building gave him the right to kick us out, gave him a reason to put the police on the trail of people who already had records.

"Right now," Michaud said, "you are living a comfortable life. You lie to yourself; you pretend you are one of them — not just a human, but a bohemian as well. But Maurice ... you know that you are more like me than you admit."

"Fuck you."

"And you swear in English now? How quaint."

We stared. Then Michaud stood. He shrugged on his jacket and buttoned it, top button only.

"I do not expect you to open the doors to your mind right here and now. Despite our surroundings, it would not be proper. You are a Frenchman, after all. My team does not need to witness such indignity."

I glared. *Indignity*, it would be. Lying down to let someone pilfer your memories is like lying down and spreading your legs.

"Next Thursday," he said. "That is when the bulldozers will come and destroy all you have, or all you pretend to have. That is when you will give me what you've stolen — or else you go free, while all the others suffer."

EIGHTEEN
TASSE DÉBORDANTE

Annabel waited for more.

"I don't understand," she said.

"He was blackmailing me," Maurice explained. "If I didn't do what Raphael wanted, he'd ruin the lives of all my friends."

"Why not ruin *your* life?"

Maurice tipped his head. "Two reasons, I think. The first is that a vampire's life — especially one as seasoned and as strong as me — is considerably harder to ruin than that of a fragile human. But second, he knew my friends meant more to me, at that time, than I meant to myself. With Celeste out of my life, I was kind of a piece of crap in the '8os, and I knew it. I was totally nihilistic. If my world ended, that was something I could accept. But when he threatened Jess, Stacy, Anarchy Jim, and God knew who else? They were all confused kids just beginning their lives. I couldn't let the Gordon Gekko of vampires ruin them just because *I'd* come around."

Annabel nodded, understanding. This, for Maurice,

was already a pattern. When he'd told her about Chicago during the 1920s, he'd felt guilty for derailing the human family he and Celeste had stayed with. Those people had been steered into the vampire world because Maurice had chosen their home as shelter, then died for the same reason. Guilt was one of Maurice's strongest levers. Strange for a vampire.

Annabel's eyes went to the clock, then promptly forgot it. Time didn't matter. Something told her that her husband wouldn't mind if she came home late. In the stillness she seemed to hear his voice, confirming it: *Askth him.*

"I get that you were blackmailed," she said. "What I don't understand is what Raphael wanted from you." She flipped through her pad, trying to find a note. It took longer than she expected, in part because she didn't really recall many of the notes she'd taken. Looking through them now, they struck her like something written by another hand. "What exactly is a ... a 'tassie whatchacallit' anyway?"

"A *tasse débordante* is a human whose mind been converted into a living databank," Maurice explained. "The term means 'overflowing glass.' They can be stuffed with information until it seems they might spill over. In English, they're simply called 'vessels.' Vampires can't be vessels; our brains are fixed when we turn and can't form new connections. Learning to be a *tasse* is incredibly tricky, requiring years to do right. The system is like mnemonics, only better: the kind of thing memory athletes do, only much more thorough. More practical, too. You can actually store *concepts* in a vessel, not just trivia like the order of a deck of cards. The whole thing is a lost art, though. No one does it anymore. Today, if you wanted to store a vessel's worth of information, you'd just make a big computer file, encrypt it, and hide it on the Dark Web. Before modern computing, though, vessels were the only reliable way to store large amounts of information you didn't want anyone else to find."

"You couldn't just write it down?" Annabel asked.

"Writing can be discovered and used against you. Storing information inside a human mind is far safer. Any competent vessel can be 'locked' with a hypnotic codeword, and once locked even the vessel himself won't know what information he was carrying."

"So this ..." Looking through her notes, wondering when she'd written all this. "... this man François ... he was one of these 'vessel' people? Michaud filled his mind with information?"

"Him and me, yes. It was back when we were working together, but working together didn't last. Eventually I cut my losses and moved to New York in 1921. You know that story."

Annabel nodded. She didn't know it all, but she knew the basics. Only, there were inconsistencies. Based on what he'd said last time, she'd marked his arrival in New York as 1924 or '25, not '21. What else about it was she missing?

"I figured Raphael could keep what we'd begun to build. What did I care? I just wanted out, and Celeste was at her limit. So we left. We just vanished, as quietly as we could."

"He could 'keep what you'd begun to build.' What was that, exactly?"

"It was a power play, is the simplest way to describe it. Very Raphael."

"Very him, but not you?" Annabel said.

"He was always driving the ship, but yes, it was half mine. Building something as complicated as we did required a lot of records, a lot of info to keep track of. We started storing proprietary information inside François: patentable inventions, processes, all things that made sense for legit businesses just trying to get by. After that Raphael expanded into information harvesting. He hired spies — *vampire* spies, whose memories could be directly viewed by those who shared their blood — to scope our competition. More blackmail, basically. He managed to get insider information on half the people up and down the Siene, inside the intelligence agencies, politicians, titans of industry.

"There were two prongs to Raphael's plan to become giants: We had to build our empire, but we also had to ruin the competition. That, we'd do either by forcing them out or stealing what made them special — a tactic Raphael was by then quite good at. That part of things rubbed me wrong from the start. It was one of the things we fought about. I was already seasoned. I had my wealth and had seen the world. I had so much abundance, I've forgotten all the places I squirreled it away. I didn't see the need to bulldoze and manipulate, because I knew what we were making would get where we wanted it in time. But for Raphael, the whole thing was a matter of pride. He didn't want money, really. Still doesn't, 'moolah' or no moolah. Money — like political connections or fame or acres of land owed or number of women bedded — is just one more way for him to keep score."

"In the end ..." Annabel flipped pages, her tone thoughtful. "Well, what *does* he want?" she asked.

"To win, of course."

"Win what?"

"Anything. Everything. If you had him on this couch, you'd have so much fun if he decided to let you live. Something broke the man a long time ago. I don't know if he even has an ego of his own. I think he borrows ego — *appropriates* it, might be a better word — from the world, always wondering what would impress it most. In the end, all that matters is that Raphael Michaud comes out on top."

Annabel considered. Yes, that sounded about right. Her knowledge of Michaud was scant, secondhand, and hearsay, but from Maurice's description he sounded so insecure as to be dangerous. The way Maurice described his clothing, his car, his office's location, and the venue in which he'd chosen to meet, Michaud sounded to her like a man in pursuit of symbols of wealth more than wealth itself. He didn't need to actually be rich and powerful, so long as the world — and Michaud himself — felt he was.

"So you left France. You left this ... was it a business? ... behind."

Maurice nodded. Annabel wasn't sure it *was* a business, but the nod was all he gave her.

"But Raphael was upset, that day in Austin, because François left France, too," Annabel went on. "And without François, Raphael couldn't actually *run* the business you left him — not after the French FBI or whoever cracked down on him. He didn't have all the information he needed to do what needed doing, because it was locked up in François's head."

Maurice nodded again. "Right. Without all his blackmail fuel, the *police judiciare* saw their opportunity to shut Raphael down. The way I hear it, he barely survived. But he's scrappy, so he *did* survive. And he flourished, here in the New World."

Annabel thought, tapped her pad with her pen, and recrossed her legs.

"And you say that when you left for America, François followed?"

"Celeste and I left as quietly as we could. Vessels, once

imprinted, can't be far from those with the keys to their mind. If it goes on too long, they go mad. They can get away with being separated for a few weeks, maybe a month. No more. So whenever and whyever François decided to cross the ocean, he did so at a substantial risk: leaving Raphael behind in the hopes of finding his other key-holder. He might not have been able to find me. But he must have, if he lived."

"And you never knew?"

Maurice shook his head. "He must have gotten a place close to where I settled. Within a mile is usually good enough. Vessels don't need to interact with their creators; they just need to stay within a radius. I moved to New York and he moved to New York. I moved to Chicago and he moved to Chicago. I understand why Raphael thought I'd taken him with me, but I didn't. That day in the Driskill was the first I'd heard of François since I set sail."

"Why, though? Why wouldn't he just stay where he was, and know he was safe?"

"Because even if he was safe, he wasn't happy," Maurice answered. "You need to keep vessels alive and you need to keep them healthy, but you don't have to be nice to them. You don't have to give them opportunities or ensure they have good lives. Raphael was paranoid that François might abscond with all we'd stored inside his head, so he used to lock him up like a prisoner. I always let him free. I knew he'd stick around — I mean, for fuck's sake, he'd go nuts if he didn't. But being a vessel is different from being glamoured, and François was always lucid. Just a man, really. And *as* a normal man, he hated Raphael and liked me. When he learned that I was gone, I guess he figured he'd rather stay close to my mind than to his tormentor's, if he had to be near one of us. He probably got a normal job and had a normal life, living out his days staying near me like a power source. I found out later that he died of natural causes, leaving three children and a lot of grandchildren who I finally met just a few years back. That pleased me more than you might imagine."

Annabel could imagine plenty. Over the course of just two sessions, Maurice had revealed a surprising amount of compassion — for others, if not for himself. Two thousand years undead hadn't hardened him. It had let him see all of transient life's more subtle facets, which seemed more real to him than the plastic feel of eternity. If he'd seen one man abused and then escape to live happily, it was no shock to Annabel that it would please him.

"So he gave you an ultimatum," Annabel said. "Michaud, I mean."

"Yes. It's possible to empty a vessel's contents into a less secure medium, if there's reason to do so. He probably figured that when François got old, I'd taken him apart to keep what was in him, just in case I needed it. By then, though, I had no interest. I'd had my fill of empire-building."

"Why did he wait so long? Why was it 1985 before he came to you?"

"That's part of the story. You'll see."

"Was he looking for you?"

"I'm not sure. Knowing Raphael, he probably never *stopped* looking."

"Were *you* looking?"

"Definitely not. Raphael Michaud, with all his pettiness and thievery and total lack of loyalty, was exactly the kind of vampire I hated most. His type was the reason I left France, New York, and then Chicago. I think I told you about the vampires who attacked my newest progeny, Reginald? The ones who I'm sure have reported back to the Vampire Council, soon to cause all sorts of trouble and probably make me and Celeste and Reginald run all over again? That's the type. These days, with all the bureaucracy and training and testing in the modern vampire world, it seems like the only type this country has."

"So you just ended up in the same city. Without planning it. Without either of you knowing the other was there."

"Right."

"And you were just a punk, tagging billboards, while Michaud was building towers downtown? Is that how it was, Maurice?" She heard the sarcasm in her voice, noted to take it down a peg — and still the voice inside pushed her on.

"He was gentrifying," Maurice said, head bobbing. "Betraying the city's promise to 'keep Austin weird.'"

Annabel stared at her pad, biting her lip. When Maurice looked at the ceiling, she looked at Maurice. Something didn't fit. Maurice and Raphael hadn't just ended up in the same place at the same time from half a world away; they'd met as neatly as if it'd been pre-ordained. His description of what had driven him and Jess to invade the Fleur-de-Lis nest had sounded almost random. *All* of what he'd said sounded random: the things that happened in the right place at the right time, steering them in the right directions. But wasn't it all just a little too coincidental?

Annabel — or was it the voice whispering directions inside her head? — didn't think Maurice was telling the whole story.

Puth harder, said the voice.

But no. This was still delicate. It would still take time to extract, like encryption in the mind of a *tasse débordante.*

Maurice's voice, surprising her out of her reverie: "Where was I, anyway?"

"You said he gave you a week to hand over what had been inside François's head, but that you couldn't because you didn't have it."

Maurice nodded and said:

With no solution and no way to fill Raphael's demand, I did the only logical thing: I kept it to myself, hoping it'd go away. Jess and Jim and a few of the others knew I'd gone to the Driskill to meet a representative of Fleur-de-Lis — our new landlords — but not my backstory with its owner, not the fact that he'd ordered me to give him something I didn't have and couldn't get. Only Jess knew Michaud's name, and I didn't plan to tell her more. She knew I was withholding and tried to get the story out of me. I told her the meeting had been nothing. I told her Raphael had just wanted me to know he was still the boss of me, and to put all of us in our places. "So this has nothing to do with that kid Daniel getting turned?" she asked me. "Nothing to do with that sense you've felt of being surrounded? Nothing to do with our little mix-up with the police or fire department?" And I told her: *No. Nothing to do with that stuff at all.* Coincidences sometimes happened; don't blame me.

I don't think she bought it. She was smart and nosy and I was never good at keeping feelings inside. I did try to solve the problem, but only in the privacy of my closet away from

Jess's snooping eyes. It hardly mattered; there wasn't a solution to be had. I hadn't seen François in sixty years. I hadn't set him down and methodically unspooled all that was inside his head, recording it on phonograph cylinder (or, later, cassette) for future reference. I hadn't found a new human, trained him or her as a *tasse* — something I didn't have a clue how to do — and transferred the archive into a new host as François was dying. I didn't have his brain on ice. So what exactly would telling the others have done? It was moot. In a week, we'd have music to face. In the meantime, it felt like waiting for the inevitable. Why ruin the week chasing something that couldn't change?

But then, after four days of silence and doing nothing and Jess bothering me that *come on, he must have said* SOMETHING, an incident occurred that changed the game.

Friday night, Anarchy Jim and I hit the Whiskey Dick during what they called pre-roll, before the club filled and bands took the stage. We had a beer. Just two dudes, acting like blue collar Joes. Or *Jims*, as it were.

"So what does it mean," Jim said, "that fucking Fleur-de-Whatever bought the block?"

He was drunk. I wasn't sure it was a real question.

"Maurice!"

"Yeah, Jim."

"You're French."

"Okay."

"Why are your people ruining the city?"

"To be fair, just one guy is ruining the city."

Jim threw up.

"I don't like it," he said when he was done.

Thinking of the vomit, I said, "I don't like it, either."

We walked out. We'd be back for the show, but they

hadn't even begun sound check. Our plan was to run back to the squat, chill a bit, then return to the Whiskey Dick. When we did, Jim would bring his camera. He wanted to interview the bands. I figured I'd go along. With four days passed since my meeting with Michaud, a lot of the menace had faded. I knew we'd be evicted; Michaud might call the cops. I didn't see how my actions tonight could change that. Might as well have fun at a hardcore show.

When we got within sight of our building, we saw the strangest thing: Drag Worm Ian, outside in the dark lot, failing to walk through the door.

We watched him for a while.

"He knows the door's open, right?" Anarchy Jim asked. He was wearing sunglasses. In my memory, Jim is always wearing sunglasses, even though I never saw him in the sun.

I looked where he'd looked. Turns out, Jim wasn't seeing half of it. My vision was orders of magnitude better than his, and I could see that Ian wasn't drunkenly stumbling into the doorframe. He was smack in its center. The door wasn't merely unlocked; it was open all the way — broken, still, from the fireman's axe. In front of Ian was a rectangle of empty space, and yet his nose was against it, making no progress, as if there were a pane of glass at the opening. His feet were moving. They pushed forward, then moonwalked backward. An invisible hand at his chest, preventing entry.

"Shit," I said, running forward.

Jim followed. I've gotten used to running at human speed by default, so he was just a second behind.

"Ian, dude," Jim said. "Having trouble getting through space, buddy?"

"I'm hungry," Ian said. He looked at Jim. "Are you ... Are you *him*?"

"Who?"

"Jesus."

"Maybe?" Jim said, asking the world.

Ian pointed, realizing. "Wait. I know you. You're Anarchy Jim!"

"I sure am. Are you high, dude?"

But Ian wasn't high. He was farther gone than that.

"Ian. Look at me," I said.

He did.

"Try again to go inside."

I pushed when he didn't move on his own. Ian's shoulder went through the doorway. Then an impossibly strong force pushed him back at me.

"The devil is keeping me out," Ian said.

Jim turned to me. "What's wrong with him, man?"

I snapped my fingers. "Ian. Did you eat?"

"Sort of."

"What do you mean, 'sort of'?"

"It got away."

Jim looked at me, but based on what I'd seen in the past, Ian's behavior was no surprise. They all have problems at first. Reginald's meals got away for weeks, until he learned to think around the problem.

I beckoned. "Jim. Come over here."

He came.

"I need your neck."

"Okay. Just give it back, dude."

I reached into my pocket. In those days I used to carry a balm of local anesthetic mixed with wax, then shoved into a repurposed Chap-Stik tube. I didn't like my human meals to feel pain, just like I didn't want Jim to feel it now.

I rubbed the balm onto Jim's neck. "You'll feel a little pinch."

"Why?"

"Because Ian is going to bite you."

That woke him up. Anarchy Jim jerked away and stared aghast.

"What the fuck?"

"I'm sorry," I said. "I thought you saw what was going on."

"And what the hell *is* going on?"

"He's a vampire. Look." I reached for Ian's lips, then pulled the top one back. As hungry as he was, of course his fangs were descended.

"What the shit, man!" Jim startled back, then recovered. Quieter, he said, "But he lives on the Drag, in the sun!"

But that wasn't true anymore, was it? Not recently. Not since he'd come to us in pain, laid down on our couch, and slept for days. He'd caught a little burn before the process was complete, moving around just half-nocturnal, but if he remained outside when the sun came up now, he'd fry. My guess was that he'd gotten up, gone hunting, and had crossed the final vampire threshold while out. Now a vampire, he couldn't get back in.

"I'll bet he was turned last week," I said, inspecting. "Most people don't flip as fast as Daniel did. For most, it takes time to go all the way. Vampires can't enter human homes without permission. Remember how I told you that when Leigh delivered all that paperwork, she included a note? The note gave me Leigh's permission to enter this building. Her name must be on the paperwork." I looked back at Ian's lack of progress. "This must be a human home now, if it's keeping uninvited vampires out."

"How could Ian go inside before?"

"Until a few days ago, they didn't own it."

"How could *you* be here before?"

"It's complicated," I said. "Vampire lore is tricker than

tax law. Before Fleur-de-Lis bought it, the building was owned by the bank. Banks are corporations. Corporations aren't people."

"Fuckin' A they're not!" Jim said, idealism trumping shock. "Corporations got no souls!"

"If the bank had been an LLC, I might have had a problem, but C-corps aren't a problem. Don't ask. I don't make the rules, and don't know who does." I looked up and down our crapped-out building. "It must be owned by Leigh now. Not Michaud. Human owner. See?"

Together we watched Ian try to enter. The invisible force pushed him out. He didn't stop, though. He kept mindlessly marching like a sleepwalker on a treadmill..

Jim leaned in. I swore he sniffed Ian, like a curious dog might.

"He's a *vampire?*"

"Yeah."

"How?"

"I don't know. Someone turned him. Maybe if we can get him lucid, we can ask him. He's pretty messed up." I reached out, waved a hand in front of his eyes, got no response. "Sometimes a person's state when they're turned carries through to vampire life. Ian was tripping on acid when he was turned. If that's the problem, he might be high forever. But these same symptoms show up in vampires who are very weak, their bodies essentially dying. We call it 'blood delirium.'" I watched Ian try to march, still not making progress. "We can't get him inside the building. Not unless we want to take a trip to see Leigh Everness and get her permission. But we *can* help Ian feel better — and if we do that, maybe we can learn a few things."

"*Help him,*" Jim repeated. "Okay ... how?"

I held up the Chap-Stik for him to see. Wiggled it. He

couldn't know what it was, but he'd catch my meaning from context.

Jim's face betrayed disgust. "Does he really need to *bite* me? Isn't there a way to do it that's like ... like donating blood or something?"

"Well, there's a device that clean-freak vampires use for transferring blood, called a Belligrand—"

"Yeah. Cool." Jim snapped and pointed in my face. "That's it. Use a Bellthingy."

"—but I have no idea where to find one. Only tightasses use them."

"I got no problem being called a tightass."

"Tightasses like our landlord, Raphael," I elaborated. *"He'd* use a Belligrand. He used to have meals extracted from humans with a syringe."

"OH, FUCK THAT GUY!"

I nodded. Manipulating Jim was too easy. *Be like The Man? No way!*

Still reluctant, he came toward me. I worked the anesthetic over his carotid artery.

"This is gross," Jim said.

"Some humans find it erotic."

"I'm not erotic for Ian, dude."

"Then just be erotic for learning the truth, if we can get him feeling better."

"The truth. Yeah. I guess I *am* erotic for that. I've got a big, purple, veiny boner for the truth."

"That's the spirit."

Bite. Suck. I stayed ready to pull Ian off if he didn't stop on his own. I didn't need to worry. Ian finished quickly, his new system still unable to process much blood. For now, he'd probably split his consumption between blood and human food. The latter wouldn't nourish him, but he'd take it by habit. That's how it is for all vampires at first — or, in Reginald's case, stubbornly forever.

I gave Jim a cotton patch and some medical tape — more goodies from my feeding kit. He pressed it to his neck. I handed a paper napkin to Ian.

"Ian," I said.

For the first time in days, he looked at me with sanity in his eyes. They were new eyes. I could see them sparkle, fathoms deep. Vampire eyes. Eyes without the usual soul, harboring an older soul instead.

"*Maurice?*" He looked to Jim, rubbing his neck with the patch. "What happened to you?" he asked.

"Serious?" Jim looked at me. "Is he serious?"

"Blood delirium," I repeated. Then to Ian: "How do you feel?"

He didn't answer right away. It took a second, because the answer he felt was so much different from the answer he expected..

"Really good," he finally said. "Amazing, in fact. Was I high?" Another deluded look around. "Am I high right now?"

Poor ignorant bastard. He'd lost days, I was sure. So much was about to change.

"We need to talk," I told him.

He started for the building's door. I stopped him inches from embarrassing himself again.

"At the Whiskey Dick," I said. "Come on."

TWENTY
TURNED

I laid it out. Ian took the news better than most. I think the way he saw it, he was already living a counterculture life. Vampirism was just a different kind of counterculture, and this one came with superpowers.

"You can't go back to the squat," I said. "You'll have to sleep somewhere else."

"Like your mom's house," Anarchy Jim suggested. He'd been barely paying attention for the past half hour, as the first band began toting its gear onstage. The case containing his camera was beneath the table. I kept wanting to tell him to just take it and go; be a star-fucker with his interview scheme already.

"No. Not there. I've always hung out with my people on the Drag, right? I believe in the streets, not the system. I'm like you guys."

Jim wrinkled his nose at that, but not because Ian stunk. He'd stopped stinking the moment he'd turned — something about vampire blood, that sexy aura we project, or the fact that bacteria run from our bodies as quickly as they can. It was only his clothes that had held the odor, and we'd thrown him new ones from Roland's closet. Now he looked like a poseur: a deadbeat Drag Worm in a Black Flag t-shirt, and not just *any* Black Flag shirt. It was the red Slip It In number with the nun on it doing ... well, I could never tell what that nun was doing. Humping a naked leg, maybe.

"You can't live on the Drag anymore," I said. "The sun will kill you."

"They say everything will kill you these days."

"I'm being literal. You go into the sun, you fry."

Ian cocked a finger and said, *"Riiiight"* in a way that made me think he didn't actually understand, and thought I was making a weirdly lewd suggestion.

Fast forward, and Ian ended up living in the sewer. There was a loose manhole cover in the middle of 38th Street right outside our building. We checked it out and decided he could spend his days there. It was disgusting. Ian, used to the "comforts of the street" seemed to take it as a challenge.

We asked him questions. Mostly me.

"Do you know who turned you?"

Ian thought. "Not sure. How would I know?"

"It'd be someone whose blood you drank."

Jim retched.

"I don't remember drinking anyone's blood."

"Think hard."

"I feel like that's something I'd remember, Maurice."

I considered pushing, then let it go. Often, new vampires had blind spots — their hybridizing minds' way of protecting their sanity.

"Do you know who turned Daniel?"

"How would I know *that?*"

I had a theory, but Ian wouldn't get it if I explained. If the same vampire turned him and Daniel, Ian would have his maker's blood memories even if he didn't quite know how to access them. If he'd free-associate, he might find it subconsciously.

"Just think. Or, better: Don't try to find an answer. Just make something up."

"You want me to *make up* the story of Daniel getting turned?"

Halfway. What I actually wanted was to trick his mind into giving up its gold. "Go for it," I said.

He wasn't sure how to proceed, but in time we got him rolling. He spun the tale of an affectionate encounter between Daniel and "some guy" at the Whiskey Dick, how it'd moved out to the loading dock when things got serious, then how lust had turned to violence and injury. It must have been like vampire rape: the maker forcing his blood on Ian after taking Ian's blood for his own. I asked Ian to describe the one who'd turned Ian — hence, probably, the one who'd turned him. That's when Jim got overenthusiastic and jumped in.

"It was Leonardo, wasn't it?" Jim elbowed me. "Describe Leonardo for him, Maurice."

"Who's Leonardo?"

"Sorry: Donatello."

"I don't know what you're talking about, Jim."

"Well goddammit, it was *one* of the Ninja Turtles!"

I understood. He meant Raphael. But I knew that was wrong; Raphael was a germophobe and a lot of other kinds of phobe. He donor blood from a glass, not a neck. He wouldn't go into a basement, eat snacks from a common bowl, open a doorknob without a hankie, or go near a spider. If there'd been a playground at this point in our lives,

Raphael would be pushed down by bullies on it. Then he'd engineer a hostile takeover and liquidate all the bullies' pensions.

I steered Ian another way. Instead of Raphael, I described Adam — the hawk-faced vampire I'd seen that night in the nest and again at Raphael's side in the Driskill bar. At that, Ian nodded right away, adding details of his own.

That meant Adam had turned Daniel.

And, almost for sure, Adam had turned Ian.

But why? What was the point? To scare us? To intimidate us into leaving? I asked Ian, just in case he'd gotten a feel for his maker's intentions, or anything else that might point to motive.

Ian didn't know. Nothing rang a bell. He and Anarchy Jim and I looked at each other across the table while the band strummed and tested the mics in the background. The walls in here were painted black, their finish chipped by the collisions of a million wasted punkers. The place was home, full of comforts. This strange thing, upon us so suddenly, sullied them.

"I ... I keep thinking of a woman," Ian said as he searched his mind. "Who's the woman?"

I already knew where this was going. I sat up straighter, dots threatening to connect.

"What woman?"

Leigh, I thought at him. *The woman is Leigh Everness, Michaud's 25-year familiar.* But what about her? How did she play into all of this?

"She said ..." Ian's face scrunched. It's like he hadn't heard me. "She said to that Adam guy ..."

"What, Ian? *What* did she say to Adam?"

Ian was focused inside, trying to tune into his blood.

"She said to go feed the keeper," he told us.

"The keeper?"

Now Ian looked up at me. "She told Adam to go downstairs," he said carefully, handling the idea like something fragile, "and 'feed the keeper of the cellar.'"

TWENTY-ONE
THE KEEPER OF THE CELLAR

In my mind, I saw rows and rows of bottles. A dim space, cool and temperature controlled. For a while I couldn't tell whether the memory was my own or someone else's. In the past I'd seen similar places and felt similar vibes. I'd been in other dim, cool places filled with bottles, hearing the strange muted echo that only happens below ground. The new memory was now, in the moment, entangled with the old one. Was I truly in Austin in 1985? Or was I across the sea a hundred years earlier?

I thought: *The Keeper of the Cellar.*

François. François had called himself that. It'd been our thing, between he and I. We'd both loved wine, but unlike Raphael we'd loved spending time in the must of earth to discuss it. François was our vessel, but while his brain held our information, his hands still needed something to do. So we'd given him chores, some of which he'd hated and been paid for, some of which he'd done out of love. Tending the wine cellars had been the latter — and something I (not Raphael) shared with him.

I was the kind one of our ruling twosome. Raphael was

the brute. Raphael used to order François around, whereas I asked politely. Raphael employed fear; I tried for kindness. Because of it, François and I had bonded in the most natural way: I was the one he liked, whereas Raphael was the one he loathed. We conspired together, talking behind Raphael's back, spending long hours among the bottles because the cellar was one place Raphael would never come. When he wanted a bottle from the cellar, Raphael sent someone for it. There were too many spider webs down there for him. Too much earth. Too much dirt, and muck, and things that ran on many skittering legs.

Monsieur Michaud may be an ass, François once told me with a smirk, *but it is I who control his most valuable asset.* He'd waved his arms theatrically, indicating our expansive collection. *He is the connoisseur of this home's wine, yes — but true power lies with me: the Keeper of the Cellar.*

Inside Ian's blood memory, Leigh Everness had told the maker, *Go feed the Keeper of the Cellar.*

Sixty or seventy years back, that would have translated to, *Feed François.*

But François was dead. Living, he'd be nearly a hundred. She couldn't have been talking about him, could she? How could anyone go feed a dead man only Michaud and I had known? How could they, in 1985, have been taking care of a captive that Raphael wanted *me* to find?

The answer was simple: *They couldn't be.* Either Ian was wrong or Leigh had meant some other keeper, some other cellar. Still, I couldn't shake the feeling that my hunch was right. But if it was — if François really was still alive, and if they had him confined and in need of tending — then why had Raphael made his threat? Why was he demanding that I deliver François or his memories if François was already in his possession?

In my own head — not Ian's this time — I heard another line from long ago:

A bottle this fine should not be consumed with the lips and tongue. It must be consumed with all the soul, on the heels of a conquest.

He'd been speaking of the 1787 Chateau Lafite. The thought gave me a shiver and filled me with guilt. I never thought I'd hear that voice again. Or sense that presence. Or feel its proximity, in the curious way of knowing someone is beside you without needing to turn your head.

It wasn't right. It was a voice and presence out of time.

I sat on my disturbed ponderings until Saturday. Until Sunday. As paralyzed as I'd been after my meeting with Michaud, this was a hundred times worse. I ignored it until Monday. Until Tuesday. Shockingly, nothing improved. I didn't know what to do. If Raphael really did have François, that meant the rest of this was a game. I was supposed to react one way to his threat, whereas the truth had me considering another. Why? What was he really playing at, waiting all this time to spring on me, then sending me on a wild-goose chase for something he already had? And what was I supposed to make of his possession of the *tasse* after all these years? It'd been dangerous in his hands back in the 1800s and was twice as dangerous now. The information in it was outdated; that much was true. But the weaknesses our transgressions exposed had deepened with time — aged like a fine wine, you might say. Inside that archive, we'd stored behind-the-scenes knowledge of society's most precious structures. We knew where famous bodies were buried ... literally, in many cases.

I could only imagine how the information in that archive, if released, might unseat history.

I could only imagine the tumult some of it might cause, if it hit the papers.

So on Tuesday, after accepting that I couldn't just sit by and hope for the best, I ran to Michaud's building. I went on foot and under the cover of darkness — not to the den we'd entered before, but to the temple he'd built to Fleur-de-Lis with its windowless, vampire-friendly floors. I wanted to burst through the front doors and cause a ruckus. That's how uneasy I felt, still hung over from Ian's visions.

I wasn't surprised to find the building open and active after dark on a weeknight. I'd done some poking into Fleur-de-Lis during my procrastination: running by its offices when I could, peeking in windows, scoping the building. I had Jim run by in the daytime, taking his camera to record for me to see, asking him to poke and prod at the reception desk to get a feel for how the building operated when the sun was up. Near as I could tell, Fleur-de-Lis ran 24/7. In the daytime, the humans did their deals. At night, the real powers took over.

Security was a large man with a nametag that read SCHMIDT. Human, by the smell.

He stood. Put a hand out. He'd stop me if he had to, but he'd try politeness first.

"Good evening, sir. How can I help you?"

"I want to talk to Raphael Michaud."

"Mr. Michaud is unavailable right now."

That was rich. My acute ears had heard his chortling laugh from outside, shouting, somehow inebriated. It's hard for a vampire to take enough of a substance to end up drunk or high unless it's Thrilloglobin, but Raphael had always managed. While Schmidt and I faced off, I heard him laugh again from deeper in the building.

"My name is Maurice Toussant," I said. "I'm his—"

"I'm sorry, Mr. Toussant. He's not available."

"I know he's in the building. I can hear him. Why don't you just go tell him I'm here?"

"I have instructions not to bother Mr. Michaud, sir."

I fixed the guard with my eyes. He looked away, then fished behind his back. He came out holding silver handcuffs. Even a foot from my skin, I could feel the loathed metal repelling me.

"Please don't attempt to glamour me, sir. I have training to prevent it. If you persist, I'll have no choice but to restrain you."

I found my temper rising. After finally psyching myself up for this confrontation, I'd be damned if I'd walk away from Human Schmidt now.

"I should warn you," the guard said as he saw me thinking, "there are silver-threaded security doors on the stairwell and before the elevators. Our halon system sprays silver nitrate. If you attempt to get past me ..."

I assessed Schmidt's eyes. Should I try to glamour him anyway? But no — he was meeting my gaze, almost like a challenge. He wouldn't need to resist my glamour for long. Just long enough to hit the alarm.

Just kill him, said the voice in my head.

But if the doors were silver-threaded and the overhead nozzles sprayed nitrate, maybe trying wasn't the best of ideas.

I looked back at the door through which I'd come. At some point, Schmidt or an automated system had lowered a sliver mesh over it, like a screen door any human could go through but that would leave me in a puddle of sweat.

There was mesh over the windows, too — there all along or lowered just for me, I wasn't sure.

"I can leave a message for Mr. Michaud," the guard said, "if you'll agree to leave peacefully."

But the door to the elevator at the lobby's far end opened before I could answer. A woman emerged, and she didn't seem surprised to see me squared off against the doorman at all.

She was blonde, forties, overbite, commanding in every sense of the word.

"Please, Jonah," she said, "put away your toys and let Mr. Toussant through. We've been expecting him."

TWENTY-TWO
FAMILIAR

She led me into an office full of windows. Her office, I had to assume. This was my first time meeting Leigh Everness, but after all the back and forth I felt like I knew her. I'd gotten a mental picture of the kind of person able to be Raphael's familiar, and Leigh's manner wasn't far off. Familiars aren't like prey or the glamoured. Their purpose is to conduct a vampire's affairs when he or she cannot — and while that makes them similar to assistants, employees, or even slaves, their subservience is counterbalanced with power. Familiars must know all their masters' secrets to do their jobs, and hold all the keys. They're like the right-hands of emperors: powerful even behind the scenes.

Anyone able to play that role for Raphael Michaud would be ... well, she'd be exactly like Leigh struck me now.

Strong.

Accepting no bullshit, allowing no leeway.

Arrogant, maybe, to match his arrogance.

"Sit. Please," she said.

We were in her domain. I could snap her neck if I wanted, but I'd seen what the building had in store for rule-breakers: silver security barriers, silver nitrate from the overheads. I had power over Leigh in that I could end her — but she had power over me in that if I did, I'd never do anything again.

So I avoided the obvious power play, knowing she and Michaud made the rules. I'd end up sitting anyway, so I sat now, on my own terms.

"Can I get you something to drink?"

"How about a 1787 Chateau Lafite?"

She shrugged, apparently not realizing this was a joke. "I'm sorry. I don't really know wine. But we have a wine cellar in the building, if—"

"Water is fine."

"Please, Mr. Toussant. You're among friends. I have much more interesting libations." She moved to a small refrigerator, which she opened to reveal hanging pouches of blood.

"'Strong male, 20s,'" she read off one bag. "'Virgin female,'" off another. "Or if you prefer something more seasoned ..."

"I'm okay. Really."

She shrugged, brought me water.

"Raphael tells me you have his archive. I've been hearing about it forever. Have you brought it with you today? Is that why you're here?"

I scrutinized her. Had he really shared our past with this human?

"The *tasse débordante*," she said, in case I didn't understand.

She was acting like she didn't have it. Like she didn't even know. I hadn't considered the possibility, but now that I was here it made perfect sense. She hadn't called François by his name in Ian's vision. She'd called him

"Keeper of the Cellar." Raphael must have tucked him away, then considered Leigh on a need-to-know basis. She knew Raphael claimed to want the *tasse*, but not that he'd already found it. That was just like Michaud: keeping everyone in the dark, paranoid, charging Leigh to manage François's care without giving her a clue what he truly was. Had she even seen François, or only sent lackeys to feed him the way you'd feed a neighbor's cat? Probably not. If she saw the man and intuited his value, she might ask questions.

I thought, *Play dumb. Save your truths for Michaud.*

"The *tasse* is gone," I said. "I don't have it."

"Is that what you came here to tell me?"

"To tell Raphael. I need to speak with him." I took a risk and added, "In private."

"I'm surprised the guard downstairs didn't tell you. Raphael is booked for the evening."

"Drinking and partying?"

She shrugged.

"Call him," I said.

"Apologies, Mr. Toussant, but you are not in charge here."

"He'd want to hear this. He *needs* to hear this."

"My ears are his ears. If you have something to deliver, you can deliver it to me."

"I told you. I don't have it."

She looked at her watch. "It's just after midnight. Technically Wednesday. On Thursday, your deadline expires. Unless you'd like to beg him — beg *me* — for more time?"

"More time helps nothing. Do you hear what I'm saying? *It doesn't exist anymore.*"

I was testing her. Sticking to the official story, saying words, watching her reaction. I watched her eyes flick down. We'd taken the elevator up to the 16th floor, so she might be looking toward anything.

She sat on the arm of a chair, not on its seat. I was lower, looking up. Leigh was average height, but I was no taller then than I am now. She sat side-saddle, both legs to the left.

"Why did you come here, Maurice? May I call you Maurice?"

I said nothing.

"Have you ever had a familiar, Maurice?"

"No."

"If you had, you'd know it's a partnership, like a marriage. One is nominally the master, but in practice we're equal. The relationship is founded on respect. We're two sides of the same coin. When Raphael is awake, he's in charge. When he's asleep or occupied, I am. Only, it's more than that. I actually slip into his role. I run the board. I take the meetings. I've been with him 25 years — long enough to know more of his secrets than you think you do. Now, I know it's no 'thousand years' like your marriage to Celeste, but I find it almost as respectable."

I watched her eyes, not trusting myself to respond. Whatever this had been when I'd entered, it'd just become something else. There were a hundred ways she could have known my wife's name was Celeste, or that we'd been married for almost a millennium. But to my ears, she'd said it like a threat.

"I don't mind telling you, I have a vested interest in what he's doing with you," she went on. "If what Raphael and I have is a partnership, and if he needs me just as I need him, that means we both stand to benefit from ... well, from *everything*. I'm not bound to him, you understand. Only a fool tries to glamour his familiar, or restrict them in any way. You can't control someone when you're sleeping, so the only way to build a foundation is with trust. Or, alternately, with a shared mission from which both will gain."

"You gain by being Raphael's lackey?"

Instead of taking it as the insult it was, Leigh smiled again. A little patronizing this time.

"I'm 45 this year," she told me. "These days, that's almost too old to be turned. The Vampire Council increasingly authorizes turnings of only those who are young and strong. But even when I was younger, I wouldn't have passed the Council's muster. Not if I wanted to be *official*."

This was a knock at me, I imagine. I'd only turned two vampires by then — Celeste and Daisy — and both had been turnings of consequence. This was long before Reginald, but Reginald's turning wasn't any better. I seem to make vampires purely to save their lives. It's a far cry from the way things are supposed to be done, and even in 1985 "wanton creation" was a slur. Nobody wanted to be the garbage of the vampire world. You wanted to be turned officially or not at all — especially if you cared about upward mobility.

"I had severe joint inflammation when I was younger. The doctors said my body was attacking itself. I walked with a limp — a noticeable one, and not something the Council wanted carried into eternity if I was made vampire. I finally got it under control a handful of years ago, and now I walk just fine." She paced to show me. "But now? Well. Forty may be the new thirty in the human world, but in the perfect world of vampires, it's too old. There's really only one way for me to be turned. Do you want to guess?"

"Graduation," I said. I'd already referenced it to Michaud at the Driskill.

"*Graduation*," she repeated. "25 years serving the same vampire as familiar and he's required, by law, to turn me.

It's the one time in my life that bureaucracy actually works in my favor."

"Michaud said you didn't want to be turned."

"He'd prefer I wasn't. He thinks that once I'm turned, I'll find greener pastures. In truth, I'm not that stupid. Raphael is ruthless and strong. All the green pastures I need are right here. But frankly, it's not his decision to make. 25 years and I'm entitled. He's got nothing to worry about. We'll find a new daywalker, and in the meantime I'll become the right hand he needs when he's awake — something he doesn't currently have."

I thought of Michaud's half-dozen yes-men with their suspenders. They weren't "right hands." They struck me as chuckleheads. Maybe she was right. Maybe this was for mutual benefit.

"You think you know him, but you don't," I said. "He won't turn you. He'll find an excuse to decline."

"I've put in my time. All I need is a grand gesture in service of my master. After that, the Council is required to recognize me. They even have to send a Graduation ensemble to assist."

"He'll deny your grand gesture. You'll petition the Vampire Council for a Graduation turning and they'll tell you no, Mr. Michaud didn't think that gesture was grand enough. You'll be sitting on your hands, waiting for a contingent of Council Guards who never come."

"I have my ways, Maurice. You'd be wise not to underestimate me like Raphael has in the past."

I watched her face. She was pretty, and had clearly been a beauty when she was young. If she was 45 now, she'd have been twenty when Michaud found her. There was no chance their relationship hadn't begun as a sexual one, knowing him. The way she was answering now —

paying lip service to the ideas of partnership and trust, but scheming against a roadblock she knew Michaud would put in her way — felt to me like the spite of a jilted lover.

Preemptive strike, I thought. *Take a shot before you no longer can.*

"Two of my friends were turned by someone who works with you," I said. "The maker's name is Adam."

"Interesting," she said. Meaning: She already knew.

"One's dead, though."

"Pity."

"The other, Ian, is socially undesirable. He's young and stupid and was intoxicated at the time of his turning. Whoever turned him has broken the law. Both were wanton creation. No question about it."

None of this was fazing her. She raised a hand and see-sawed it in the universal gesture for *Meh, kinda, maybe, so-so.* Wanton creation was more of a guideline than a law. It was like having a kid out of wedlock: not forbidden, just frowned upon.

"You don't mind that someone who works with you is out there creating vampires the Council would disapprove of?"

"Boys will be boys."

"What if I take it to the Council?"

Now she laughed, hard. "You're kidding. I know your record, Maurice. If you go to the Council and announce Fleur-de-Lis's wrongdoing, they'll come down on you instead. Between us and the rebel Maurice, it's clear who they'd chase and who they'd leave alone. Is this really why you came? To make an absurd threat?"

"I came because of something I saw in Ian's blood memory — or actually: the blood memory of his maker."

This finally shocked her. "You traded blood with your vampire friend?"

And yes, I had, just yesterday when I'd made up my mind to come. Swapping blood with another vampire wasn't far from having sex with them, but despite my aversion, trading with Ian had felt necessary. I needed information. I was adrift, with nobody to ask for help. Every day felt like more was at stake.

"Something's been bothering me," I went on. "I've felt like someone's been watching me — watching my whole group — for months. It's like there's been a vampire around every corner. Then a kid gets turned, kills another kid, and we end up having to kill *him*. Around the same time, Ian *also* gets turned. Someone's been sniffing around town, asking about me and my friends—"

"Your *human* friends?"

I bulldozed on without comment. "—calling the cops on us, calling the fire department, asking how to get in touch with me and where I hang out. I've been hearing about *you* for a while now: coming to my home, stalking my club, giving business cards to my friends like an Amway salesman. You're supposed to be a real estate developer. Why the hell are you bothering me?"

She opened her mouth to answer. I cut her off because I didn't really care to know.

"So yes," I said. "I traded blood with Ian. I needed to see through the eyes of his maker."

"But ... that's—!"

Illegal, offensive ... She could have finished her thought with anything. I cut her off first by saying, "—*justified? Understandable?* You've had your nose up our asses. I needed to understand, so I did."

"And?"

Go for broke. Tell her what you saw. Tell her about the memory you squeezed from Ian's maker's mind, proving this was all worthwhile.

"I know what's in your cellar."

She waited. Watched me. Bit her lip. And I thought: *She knows about François after all. She's only playing dumb.*

"What *is* in the cellar, Ms. Everness?"

She stared, challenging me. Then she said: "Wine."

"May I see it?"

"Unfortunately not. Raphael has left specific instructions that you, in particular, are not to be allowed near his wine collection."

"Why not?"

"He's convinced you're a thief."

"Are *you* allowed down there?"

"Yes."

"And Raphael, of course."

Another stare-down. She knew what I was hinting. Finally, masks were off: I knew what she knew and she knew what I knew. I thought I had a good idea what she was after. What *he* was after. What both of them, perhaps, truly wanted.

"Except that Raphael doesn't go into the cellar, does he?" I added.

The cellar. Where the prize is kept.

"This is Texas. There are scorpions down there."

"You're sure?" I asked.

"I've seen them. I mentioned it to Raphael."

I smirked. "I'll *bet* you did."

Again we locked eyes. I was saying something to her beyond my words and she was saying something right back. Neither one of us wanted to pop the bubble and say it out loud. I thought: *Do you know something?* And she seemed to answer: *Do YOU know something?* It was detente, mutually assured destruction. I only knew that Raphael was terrified of arachnids and that what she'd said was true. He avoided basements. Mention of even one spider would keep him away, no matter how much he loved his wine.

"What's in your cellar?" I asked. "*Really?*"

Thinking of the vision I'd had, when I'd peered into Ian's blood. The rows of bottles — and the other thing thing hidden in a locked room in the corner.

"Wine," she repeated, locking eyes, daring me to say more.

I did: "What else?"

There was a long pause.

Then she said, "Graduation."

TWENTY-THREE
NUT PUNCH

The next day, Wednesday, Roland raised the drape patching the broken wall of my closet in the middle of the day and shouted, "FUCK THEIR MOTHERS!"

I scooted back. The sun was on the other side, but the sun-drenched front room was leaking photons and ultraviolet, bouncing it all my way.

"Roland. Come on, man. I'm dying here." Literally, if he kept holding that drape open. The day was bright. It felt about a thousand degrees.

"FUCK! THEIR MOTHERS!"

"Whose mothers, Roland." I didn't bother with a question mark. I felt equal parts sleepy and pained. I wanted to go back to bed. And, you know … not die.

"Theirs!"

"Can this wait until sunset?"

Jim appeared at the opening. I heard, "Oh, hey, are you telling Maurice?" Then I saw his brush-cut head and sunglasses beneath my curtain as well.

"Guys," I said.

"You gotta hear this, dude," said Anarchy Jim.

"Later."

"Oh, come on, dude. You're a big, strong vampire!"

"Fuck their mothers!" Roland repeated, shoving a piece of paper at me. It was black on white, scribbled-on with a red Sharpie. A demolition notice, and request to vacate. The date on it was tomorrow.

"What is this?"

"They're closing the Whiskey Dick!"

"Too much information for too early," I said.

"Fuck them!" Roland shouted, now punching my ceiling. Hit it too hard and the ceiling wouldn't seal out the sun, either. Why had I moved here again?

I heard feet outside. It was Jess. She saw what was happening, grabbed Jim's arm in one hand and Roland's in the other, and dragged them away. The drape fell and I was blessedly back in the cool dark. I heard Jess's voice.

"I'm sorry about them," she said from beyond the curtain.

"Fuck!" Roland's voice shouted.

I stared at the paper still in my hand. It listed the land designation for the next block, the address, the venue name: *Whiskey Dick. Immediate condemnation of premises; must vacate by order of the city.* They hadn't even gotten thirty days' notice.

"You gotta do something," Roland's voice said.

"*We* gotta do something," Jim corrected.

"Later," said Jess. "There's time, later."

Feet walking away. After a few minutes, I decided I was supposed to go back to sleep. The daylight had made me tired — a self-defense mechanism against the scalding of outside.

I slept for hours, not waking once. But I dreamed. I dreamed of Leigh Everness, of her final word on parting.

What's in the cellar? / Graduation. It all fit, and I didn't like it. I'd gone to Fleur-de-Lis to confront Michaud for abducting our supposedly-dead friend, then playing games with my head by demanding that I do what he'd already done. I left knowing that Michaud *wasn't* acting; he actually *didn't* know François was in his own building's cellar. It was Leigh who'd found our old vessel alive at age 95 and somehow faked the grave Michaud had found — Leigh *and Adam,* that vampire lackey of hers. It was Leigh who'd somehow learned our secrets, maybe including my worst ones. She'd tracked down our vessel, caught him, and hidden him in the wine cellar where Raphael was too OCD to go. No wonder she was so sure the Vampire Council would grant her request to be turned. There was no question Michaud wanted François more than anything; I of all people could testify to that. Presenting François as her "grand gesture" after putting in 25 years was as sure a way as anything to assure her promotion into our undead ranks.

I dreamed of Leigh, over and over. Of François starving in that cellar, begging me for help. I dreamed of Michaud receiving his gift, then unlocking François's mind and using it to do horrible things. I dreamt of Leigh taunting me by practically confirming my old friend was in her possession, daring me to do anything about it.

And then, blessedly, I dreamed of a solution. I'd need hands to do what needed to be done; that much was certain. The only question was how to recruit those hands without revealing more than I cared to. I had many, *many* things I wanted kept secret from my punk rock friends, like my past as Michaud's partner and fellow exploitation broker. How could I get them to go on a mission with me ... *without* revealing the mission's ugly truth?

I opened my closet door after sunset to find them all looking at me. I jumped.

"Holy crap, guys," I panted, blinking off sleep.

"Sorry," said Jess.

"Sorry," said Stacy Grace.

"Fuck their mothers!" said Roland.

I climbed out. I still had the demolition notice in my hand. Jess took it, and together we went into the main room. They filled me in. The notice had been posted by someone very official-looking, presumably from the city, early in the morning. My friends had been outraged and scoping since then, making phone calls, even visiting the Fleur-de-Lis office. It was lively even in daytime. Leigh, it seemed, was still in charge.

"According to what I can find out," Jess said, "Fleur-de-Lis is totally within their right to demolish the building. It's falling down as-is. Apparently they want to build another skyscraper."

"Fuckers!"

Jess eyed Roland. Jim was close, trying to take her arm. She pushed him away, then spoke.

"What I can't figure out is why, if this is something your old buddy is doing to screw with you, Maurice ... why not just knock down *this* building?"

That answer, I knew. It was the same as why Leigh hadn't tried to trap or kill me when I went to her office: Raphael, unlike Leigh, still thought I was the key to finding François, and anyone confronting me might jeopardize his chance. Leigh's motivations were simpler. I'd paid a visit to rattle her cage, so she'd rattled mine right back. She'd known what the Dick meant to all of us, so after I'd made my threats, she'd made one of her own. Posting the notice in daylight was her way of proving she could hit me where I

TWENTY-FOUR
PLANS WITHIN PLANS

"Not just *any* wine," I said two hours later in front of the assembled room. "We're talking about a 1787 Chateau Lafite."

"'Feet'?" said Drag Worm Ian, who'd climbed a ladder and was watching from outside through a glassless window.

"*La* Feet," Anarchy Jim told him. "That's French for feet."

I searched my pile of transparencies. I'd had them made pronto for this little presentation, which I was sharing on a projector Hardcore Sally had beaten out of a new-wave kid after he'd welched on a bet. I'd found a photo of an ultra-rare bottle more or less identical my own in a wine maga-zine at the library, which I projected now. It was in a green bottle, the markings handwritten on the glass instead of printed on a label. I repeated the name: not *feet*, but *Chateau Lafite.* Then I told the three-minute version of the story I'd told Jess the week before, about me and Michaud and our high-brow feud.

"*Stealing wine* will stop him?" Stacy said.

I nodded. "Believe it or not, yes. It will embarrass him. He'll do whatever we want just so he can get it back."

I wondered if that was true — if it'd *be* true, if that's actually what we were up to. Maybe. I almost wished we could try it. I kept my face neutral, now fervently avoiding Jess. She was the only weak link. Or, perhaps more fairly, the only link that was likely to call bullshit.

Stacy seemed to accept this. The others muttered.

I swapped the slide, now showing blueprints for the Fleur-de-Lis building.

"This is where we're headed. It's on Ladybird Lake, entrance on Caesar Chavez." I tapped the wall, indicating spots on the diagram. "The first two floors are reception and a restaurant. The ground floor has windows but the second floor does not. That means it's where the vampire VIP rooms will be. Where *Raphael* will be."

"Why?" asked Roland.

"Sunlight, idiot," said Ian. "The windowless floors are for vampires in the daytime."

"I meant, *why* is there sunlight?"

Ian was about to explain astronomy. Roland rushed to elaborate. "Why are we doing this *during the day*, I mean."

"Because there are a lot of vampires in that building, and vampires are weaker when the sun is up. Most will probably be asleep. If we're lucky, Michaud will be sleeping, too."

"And if he's not?"

I tapped the wall again. "Then he'll be here. It's actually what I expect. If Michaud were human, he'd be the guy who stayed out all night. He's vampire, so he stays up half the day — partying, feeding, drinking, making himself seen. But it's fine. I actually prefer it because if he's sleeping, he might dream ... and vampire dreams can be revealing. We'll go early so he's likely to still up. That's where I come in."

Jim looked at Jess. "Are you getting this?"

I thought she might say no ... and she wasn't *believing* it, either. Instead she nodded. "Maurice thinks Raphael might sense his presence, or that another vampire connected to his blood might sense him. We need Maurice, so he has to go. His thinking is that if, instead of being part of the mission, he just walks right up to Michaud and makes himself known, that's the best way of solving the problem. Michaud won't wonder why he senses Maurice and what he might be up to, if he's right there with him."

"Exactly," I said. "The rest is simple. I'll keep Raphael occupied while you guys head to the wine cellar. There seem to be silver screens *here* and *here*." I showed them on the blueprint. "They'd stop me, but you should be able to cut right through them — which is why we need humans to pull this off."

"The only defense is *screens?*"

"They aren't expecting a raid." I showed them more on the blueprint. "See these? Security doors. Plenty to stop a human. But they're open during business hours, so they shouldn't give you problems. That's the other reason we're doing this in daylight: the building won't be locked down for the night."

"So we go down to the cellar," Jim said, "and we just take the bottle while you occupy your buddy upstairs?"

"That's the idea."

"It sounds too easy."

"That's something people say in movies. In real life, theft *is* easy."

They conferred about this. In truth, I expected them to have a bit more trouble than I was allowing. They'd go into the cellar for the wine, explore the closed room when they couldn't find it, and find François instead. At that point I'd be able to enter the plan with plausible deniability: *I hadn't known there was some guy in the cellar. How could I?* They'd call me; I'd rush down; we'd smuggle François out and none would be the wiser. Raphael wouldn't know enough to stop us, seeing as François was Leigh's prisoner instead of his.

Jess was looking at me as if she knew. She couldn't know, but I looked away anyway.

I ran through the other transparencies I'd had made, including the part where I go with them in the light of day.

The punks nodded as I outlined my plan.

We'd begin at 7am. Just after sunrise.

TWENTY-FIVE
HEIST

A bottle this fine should not be consumed with the lips and tongue. It must be consumed with all the soul, on the heels of a conquest.

I remembered the voice as if it were yesterday. My mind went to ranks of gleaming bottles, kept free of dust by François's careful cloth. He used to be The Keeper of the Cellar. The vault in the earth used to be his finest point of pride ... and now, it was his prison.

I was at the bottom of an industrial laundry basket, covered with fresh linens. It wasn't elaborate, but it didn't need to be. Once Michaud saw me, he'd be so pleased to play cat-and-mouse that he wouldn't care how I'd entered. I kept reminding myself of that, while I was suffocating under all that heavy fabric, finding the walls of the wheeled basket to be far less sunproof than I'd hoped. They should have brought me in a box truck, backing up to the building's loading dock: metal and insulation between me and the blazing sun at all times.

"Doing okay in there?"

That was Jess's voice. I grunted but didn't answer. She

hadn't stopped throwing suspicious jabs, and now kept them coming.

"Are you too hot?" she went on. With all the towels and aprons above me — laundered supply to match those used by the building's restaurant — she sounded like her mouth was packed in cotton. The answer was *yes* — yes, I was hot as hell in the basket covered in cloth in the baking Texas sun. But I wasn't about to give her the satisfaction.

We waited on the dock, a bit cooler in the shade. I could hear them breathing: Jess and Anarchy Jim on the left, Roland and Watlin on the right. There was a second basket past them with Drag Worm Ian in the bottom, brought in case we needed blood-eyes on his maker. On the building's other side, Stacy Grace was getting us permission to deliver the linens. I'd told her a few names to drop, borrowed from paper I'd been able to see across Leigh's office and other paperwork seen through Ian's blood. If Stacy couldn't get us in, there was a Plan B. It involved breaking some necks. I hoped we wouldn't need it — but given the stakes, I was prepared to do what it took.

I heard the loading dock door unlock, then open. They wheeled me inside. When the door closed, the basket felt much cooler. I stood, blinking in the light. Ian stood in the basket beside me. Around us were the five humans: Anarchy Jim, Stacy, Jess, Watlin, and Roland.

I ran a hand through my hair, then tugged on my lapels.

"How do I look?" I asked Jim.

"Like a sellout."

I stepped to the side. There was a scratched mirror in the dock bathroom. I used it to straighten my bowtie, to fluff the ruffles of my tuxedo shirt.

"Like a fucking corporate stooge," Jim elaborated.

"It's a black tie club," I said. "There's a dress code."

"Like some douchebag," Jim replied, "hosting a telethon."

I gave myself a final glance, then turned to someone less caustic.

"Jess?" I tried.

She looked me over. "Sure. You look fine."

I measured her eyes. I wanted to ask if we had a problem — and if we did, if she'd please tell me now. She sighed, then shrugged. She knew something was up, but we were here now and everyone was counting on everyone else. Her look said, *I'll play ball now for the good of the group, then deal with you later if you fuck us.*

"Any problems?" I asked Stacy.

"No problems."

"Didn't someone escort you?"

"They buzzed the back door for us."

"No guard? Nobody watching you to make sure you were who you said?"

Stacy made a who-cares face. "We're just bringing towels." She was right; this was 1985 and people were a lot less concerned with checking IDs and sweating the foul intentions of strangers. Still, I'd expected at least some over-sight — not this no-chaperone party we found ourselves holding in the loading dock.

"Did you see the staircase?"

"It's just by the elevators."

"Where's the guard?"

"Near the door, where you described. Not by the eleva-tor, if that's what you're asking."

I wasn't asking that, precisely. I just couldn't shake the feeling that we were doing something wrong. That I'd made a mistake, or was making one now. I'd told Jim, *In real life, theft is easy.* But still: This felt too easy.

"Maurice," Jess said, closer and quieter. "What's wrong?"

"Nothing."

She looked at me, then the others. Then she waited for a lapse in the others' attention and dragged me ten feet farther.

"Seriously, goddammit. What's going on here?" she asked.

"Do you want to run through the plan again?"

"No, I want to know why we have a third laundry basket. The one you told Watlin to set aside. We've got two vampires. So what's the third basket meant to hold?"

"The wine."

"Tell me the truth, Maurice. What are we *really* here for?"

"Wine!"

She frowned and shook her head. "I'm not stupid. My mom used to do stuff like this. Something about vampires and trust. What, do you think we can't be trusted with the real plan?"

"Jess, this *is* the plan."

"You said you'd go upstairs. You told us to go to the cellar. You said, *five times*, to let you know if we find anything unusual while we're down there."

"Right. Just hit me on the walkie-talkie. It's rigged to vibrate. They won't know."

"What are we going to find that's unusual?"

"Anything out of the ordinary."

She met my eyes. "Stop lying to me, Maurice."

"I'm not lying to you."

"You are. Don't tell me again that you're not, because it'll just piss me off."

My mouth opened, unsure what to say. Then Anarchy

Jim approached, tapping his watch. "Guys? They're going to start wondering what we're doing back here."

I looked at the door that opened into the building, ultimately to the reception desk at the front and the guard beyond.

One guard.

Zero escorts.

Yes, Jim was right. They'd start wondering soon. The only question was, why weren't they wondering already?

"Guys?"

Jess met my eyes. So much left unsettled.

"I'll explain later," I told her.

"Yes," Jess said. "You'd better."

TWENTY-SIX
VAMPIRE 80S GUYS

I took the stairs. I must have gotten used to the lack of guards below, because I didn't see the one who'd walked up behind me until he wrapped a sliver line around my neck. The line had a long tail on it, and once he'd snared me, he stood back holding its end.

"Heel," he said.

It was a leash. A fucking *leash*.

The sun had already made me feel logy, even though I couldn't see it from the concrete second-floor bunker. I knew it was out there, and it made my bones feel heavy, my joints sluggish. With the silver around my neck as well, every movement hurt. My tendons were taut, brittle rubber, mechanical rather than fluid. I felt the way human culture shows the elderly: stooped by time, exhausted by the sheer idea of movement.

"I'm a guest of Mr. Michaud's," I said. It was hard even to talk.

"Oh yeah? What's your name, *Guest*?"

"Maurice Toussant."

"How'd you get in here?"

"I told you. I was invited."

The guard seemed to consider. I'd managed to declare myself with authority, and right now he was probably wondering how rude he could be to a man Mr. Michaud may or may not want treated well. But his bullshit meter was high — and, of course, accurate — so he seemed to be splitting the difference. He wouldn't pressure me on my method of entrance, but he wasn't going to "sir" me, either.

He pulled a walkie-talkie from his belt, speaking into it with partial sentences. He gave my name, inflating my story with lots of doubt ("... or so he claims ...") so the person on the other end would know he wasn't fooled. After a few minutes of back and forth, he returned the walkie back to his belt.

"Fine," he told me, the leash still around my neck. "Let's go, Fido."

We were two steps out when the staircase door opened behind us. It was Jess. She'd been wearing black jeans and a black turtleneck, presumably for all the sneaking we were supposed to be doing. She'd found a dark coat somewhere downstairs, maybe that of a worker, and all together the ensemble came close to basic black. She didn't look as formal as I did, but she'd done something to her hair before coming up, added a pin, adopted an attitude. She wouldn't stick out, and must have decided that snooping my true motives was worth the gamble.

"Who the fuck are *you?*" the guard asked.

"She's with me," I said, balancing surprise and fury.

The guard seemed supremely annoyed. He again grabbed his walkie. When he turned away, Jess and I engaged in an eye argument.

What the hell, Jess?

And she seemed to reply, *Did you seriously think I'd just let you lie to us and risk all our lives?*

She wouldn't back down, no matter how hard I stared. She didn't know what she was getting into. Just peeking through the restaurant, I could tell that almost everyone inside was a vampire. There were a few human guards, like this meathead, to safeguard the gathering should daylight intervene. Most everyone else (and I could already see it happening, as heads followed noses, sniffing in our direction) would be staring at Jess's neck, eager to eat her alive.

I moved closer.

"Run. *Now.* I can make an excuse."

But Jess, muttering from the side of her mouth, said, "Not on your life."

"You don't know how vampires are."

"The fuck I don't," she said, angry now, not even looking at me. "Tell that to my mother."

The guard finished his conversation, apparently green-lit on the topic of Mr. Toussant and Guest. He eyed Jess, daring her to step out of line, then tugged my leash forward. From the elevator area we moved into the lobby, past a hostess behind a stand, past a line of well-dressed vampires in white gloves who struck me as waiters, all of them licking their lips.

Beyond that was the restaurant proper. True to Michaud's usual bent for excess, it wasn't just a place to dine. There were human waitresses circulating in scant clothing, handing out drinks spiked with blood. Vampire eyes rose to meet us as we passed, many from tables strewn with pills amidst white dust that must be cocaine. Some sniffed, licking their fingers, wiping away powder. Greedy, gluttonous fools — beyond a second's rush, they wouldn't even feel it.

We crossed to a table, past flashing colored lights bounced our way from a stage full of strippers: women, men; the vampires didn't discriminate. I could see naked commotions in corners: diners, perhaps, enjoying themselves a bit more than Zagat endorsed. Screams punctuated well-bred laughter here and there: sexual escapades gone painful, perhaps, or the other way around. Between the white cloths strewn with elegant flatware were gaming tables: roulette, blackjack, hold-'em poker. It was as if the very idea of excess — the '80s incarnate — had drawn its own advertisement. If this room of sex, drugs, gambling, and conspicuous consumption had been on a billboard, our subvertising crew would have had a field day. I would have captioned it, *Stuff Lasts Forever* or *Live Big, Die Rich, Leave Nothing.* Anarchy Jim would no doubt write something more to-the-point: *Rich Guys Suck Camel Dong,* perhaps.

Around a table in the corner were seven people: Michaud and a half-dozen well-dressed yes-men. I wasn't sure if they were the same six from the Driskill, other than Adam — Ian's maker. They were otherwise homogenous, hard to tell apart. There was a vampire factory somewhere, and it was churning out douchebags.

The guard removed my silver leash and released Jess's arm. I immediately felt a thousand pounds lighter. The guard held a hand toward me, palm out. He said, "Stay."

I watched him go, wanting very badly to tackle him and rip out his throat. I could do it, easy. But what kind of quiet distraction would I be if I chased that impulse?

Raphael smiled. You'd never know it wasn't genuine, wasn't warm.

"Maurice! So fine to see you, my good friend. Please. Join us."

One of the anonymous vampire guys pulled out a chair.

He, unlike Raphael, didn't look welcoming. The motion was begrudging, done because he seemed to feel he had to.

Raphael was grinning at me. Then he noticed Jess, stood halfway, and reached across the table for her hand.

"And who is this? Maurice, you did not tell me you had such beautiful friends."

Jess extended her hand to match his. Raphael kissed its back. She held it there a second, kind of shook her head, then snapped it back. Natural charm without glamour, indeed.

"Jessica," Jess said.

"Lovely to meet you, Jessica." He introduced himself with too much pomp and circumstance. Only as she took the hint and sat in a second vacant chair did he do the same. I was left standing alone. I decided to sit in the chair begrudging-man had pulled for me.

"What a nice surprise," Raphael said. He grinned with a mouth full of what had to be caps. Vampires can cap their teeth just fine, but it always looks strange. When fangs descend, they knock off anything put over them, so vampire dentists usually leave the canine teeth natural. That's how Michaud's teeth were: straight, white, and tombstone-square everywhere but those natural pointers. It gave him a plastic look, like something not quite finished. "I did not expect you until this evening, when you are scheduled to deliver what you owe me. I would have invited you before then had I known you were interested, believe me." He spread his arms to indicate the entire black-tie affair. "But you are usually so uninterested in all things social. Will you join us for a glass of wine?"

There was suddenly a waiter behind me, so silent I'd had no idea he was there.

"Sir?" said the waiter. He indicated a bottle cradled in his hands.

I shook my head. Raphael's face twisted.

"But what is wrong, Maurice? There was a time when you delighted in drinking with me."

"Times have changed."

"Have they? I do not know. When we shared our last glass of wine, people were greedy for wealth, greedy for power. They were kind to others' faces, then stabbed them in the back. The thirst for blood, in those days, was always a price worth paying." He sipped from his stemmed glass. "Although, I do have to wonder: What has changed today?"

I caught Jess's eye. Already she looked like she'd made a mistake. All seven men kept staring at her — specifically at her neck. What would happen if they decided to pile on and do what they wished? I wouldn't be able to stop them — not here, not against them all, not with the security I knew had been baked into the building. Why had she followed me, other than to ruin our chances? The goal was always for me to occupy Michaud's mind — something I could have done alone and done better. Here and now, Jess was a liability. She'd come up because she didn't trust me, but how was this helping? Now she'd be food. It'd either be mission accomplished in the wine cellar or it wouldn't be — but thanks to her rash action, now either option might come with a casualty. Maybe a fatality.

I was too preoccupied with Jess and the now-imminent sense of danger to answer with the rhythm Raphael's dinner-cool tone seemed to demand. My hesitation, I knew, gave him power. I couldn't shake the feeling of walking on a tightrope. My original plan gave Michaud nothing to use against me. If he'd wanted to kill me, fine; he'd certainly had opportunities before. But now he could threaten Jess, and I knew it, and he *knew* I knew it. It was falling apart. It was all going wrong.

When I didn't answer, Raphael turned to Jess with a smirk. The '80s guys around the tables (all wearing red suspenders and blue pinstriped shirts today; seriously, it looked like a uniform) chuckled. Their boss was scoring point after point against his stupid rival. *Hooray!* There'd be much coke sniffed off a hooker's ass tonight in celebration.

"It would seem the cat has my good friend's tongue," Raphael said, again glancing at his yes-men. Eyes back on Jess, he said, "And what about you, Mademoiselle Jessica? Will *you* share our wine?"

"Is it *just* wine? Or is there blood in it?"

That was hilarious. I knew because all six of Raphael's talking heads chortled at once.

"So you know our secret?" Raphael said. "But of course you do. Knowledge is power, as they say. He who controls the secrets controls the world. Do you agree that he who knows the most wins?"

"Or *she*," Jess said.

Raphael smirked. "Quite. Such it is." He wouldn't dismiss her, not here and not now, not overtly and not with words. But just his tone was condescending, hard to miss.

Raphael snapped, gesturing with twirling fingers for the server. The man turned, finding another white-gloved waiter already with a glass in hand. He placed it before Jess. Raphael nodded, pointing down, saying go ahead. Wine filled her glass, more amber than crimson. Something fantastically old and no doubt fantastically expensive. Reds so delicate are no longer red — something Raphael knew I knew, and that I made the mistake of letting him see.

"Thanks," Jess said, "but I don't drink."

This was unacceptable. Raphael began to soliloquize,

praising the wine. It was all verbiage I knew. I refused to listen.

"Anyway." Michaud raised his glass, then tilted to peer through its amber meniscus against the white backdrop of the tablecloth. "To answer your question, there is nothing else in it. Particularly no blood — bloodsuckers that we are, *n'est-ce pas?* It is merely wine. Although one should not say 'merely' in a case such as this. For there is nothing on Earth as fine as a fine wine, and to discount its purity as 'mere' is an insult to all things. I have always made a point to sample the most delicious things life can offer." Now the look he gave Jess was less cordial, more salacious. Somehow poise made her simple black garb look nearly elegant, as if she'd planned it. Michaud was looking at her like something he'd like to unwrap. "A man of fine tastes. But then again, the world does not sit still, even for the likes of us. You must grab what you wish. A man I used to know well taught me that. Didn't he, Maurice?"

"Fuck your mother."

Michaud laughed, sipped. His cronies looked at each other and then their boss to make sure they were indeed having fun tonight, then proceded to laugh and smile and mentally compare Porches.

"Well," said Michaud, brushing at the tablecloth. "So it is. I would expect no less from the Killer."

Jess looked at me. *The Killer?* I shook it away. Stupid Raphael, talking out his stupid ass.

"Which one of you turned our friend Ian?" Jess asked.

Seven heads turned to her on swivels.

"And which one of you," she said, "turned Daniel and nearly set our home on fire?"

"Your *home*," Raphael said. He was repeating the phrase so she could hear how ridiculous it sounded — and also to remind her that if the squat was anyone's anything, it was his.

"Which one of you," Jess went on, somehow missing my darting glance to knock it off, "thought it'd be a good idea to buy two shitty blocks far from where you're building your big office towers, just so you could ruin something that has nothing to do with you?"

I felt the tablecloth move. I saw that Jess was gripping it, her fingertips white. That's when I realized: She didn't come up here to check on me. She came up here because she was pissed off. How had I missed that? It wasn't a suicide mission. Jess was too cocky for that. But it *was* a fuck-you mission, and the moment I'd gone off-script she'd decided it was high time to do the same.

But Michaud wasn't even a little perturbed — either underestimating her anger or missing it entirely. "*Mon chéri,* this is none of your concern. We are a team. What is done by one is done for all."

Now *I* laughed. The red-suspender brigade had been in the zone, listening to their fearless leader as if they might not devour him if he fell. They turned and met my eyes: a rude interloper in their midst.

But Michaud went on. "We had a deal, Maurice and I. I am simply requesting that he honor it. But because I know my friend, I similarly know that a *request* is not enough. It would not be the first time he has taken an ... *unexpected detour,* shall we say? ... and so for that reason I have simply taken out some insurance."

"So if he pays what he owes you, you won't bulldoze our club?"

Raphael sat up. He leaned forward, as if gathering us so he could speak in confidence. I'd seen this: the pompous man moving into lecture mode.

"All this concern over a few yards of cement and wood," he said. "Your 'club' has been on the edge of condemnation for years, according to the city. Similarly your 'home' is nothing but a shell, stripped and bare, without windows or protection, cold on winter nights and I assume hot as Hades in the summer. I am not blind. I am not stupid. You come here and ask who among us has intruded on your so-called life? It does not matter. You intruded on us *first*. It is not merely the spraypainting of signs, the sabotaging of our work sites. I know that it is you who have also stolen supplies. You who have deterred inspectors and staged fights for neighbors' eyes to see, in the middle of my show-ings to buyers and tenants. It should not be effective, this way you try with such petty means to stop what is inevitable — what will *always* be inevitable. So you ask, How dare we walk on your turf, borrowed that it may be? How dare I touch the people close to you, demand your compliance, and send my machines to destroy the hovels you've built atop what is mine? And in response, I ask you this, Made-moiselle Jessica: How dare *you* and your colorful friends press *me* first?"

The '80s guys all nodded their assent, mumbling success slogans. I think I heard one of them say, "Takes money to make money."

Jess stood. I stood in solidarity beside her, but I didn't like how this was going off the rails.

"You're a plague," she said. "All of you."

I'd have grabbed her sleeve if I didn't think Raphael would draw meaning from it. All we were supposed to be doing up here was distracting their minds while Anarchy Jim and the others retrieved François from the wine cellar, but that could have been done the way I'd wanted: with discussion, not conflict. I knew Jess's temper and sense of righteousness. I should have seen this coming. She didn't think ahead, for a smart girl. How, if Michaud tired of this, were we supposed to escape with our lives? I could protect us a little if they came for us, but not if they turned on the sprinklers or got out the silver. Nobody knew our weaknesses quite as well ourselves.

Michaud didn't rise, and she didn't get a rise from him. He was still sitting in his same place, flanked by vampires with $90 haircuts. As she glared down at him, he took another sip of his wine.

"Tell me, Mademoiselle Jessica. Are you angry about the shithole on 38th Street ... or is this about your mother?"

She leapt at him, paying no mind to the table between them. Jess's belly hit the wood, skidding, her hands on a collision course with his neck. Flatware clattered; silverware hit the floor; the wine toppled and began to glug vintage onto the white lawn in the gathering's center. Of course Michaud was far too fast for her; he was on his feet and laughing at the girl sprawled across all that fine food before she was fully launched. The henchmen readied themselves, teeth already down, hands becoming claws. They advanced a step on instinct, then pulled back when Michaud raised a hand. Guards were there in seconds, slow as humans, bearing silver leashes for me and strong hands to for Jess.

Michaud made *tsk-tsk* sounds with his lips pursed to a duckbill.

"Here to accept my hospitality," he asked, "or here to ruin a rather nice paté?"

Security dragged Jess off the table. Her front was smeared with goose liver. At the same time, there was a commotion from the rear: vampires trying to stop a newcomer, shoving them back with annoyance instead of fear. It was a human woman: two kinds not allowed here, in this land of fangs and dicks and the delights to please them.

"Miss. Miss? You're not allowed in here, Miss!"

Security, chasing the woman. Chasing Leigh Everness, who was having none of their macho bullshit. Wasn't this her building, too?

She was at our table a few seconds later, followed by the huffing security guard.

"I'm sorry, sir," the guard said to Michaud. He was broad across the chest, a bouncer we hadn't seen when we'd come up the stairs. "She barged right in."

Leigh and Michaud locked eyes. I sensed an old argument, held in abeyance for now. It was clear she didn't like the Boys' Club in general, but *really* hated being kept out of it.

"Ms. Everness is always welcome here, Stefan," Michaud told the guard. "Although ... she might have chosen a more appropriate time and method of entry."

Leigh waited for him to finish speaking, then for judgment to pass. She'd barged in for something important and seemed to resent this ritual of reprimand. She'd seen me and Jess at the table, but I'd only gotten a quick look. In that look, I'd seen no surprise.

In fact, now that her irritation was past, I saw she was smiling. *Smiling.*

There was more commotion from the restaurant's front. Leigh had been the engine of an intrusive train, and the remaining cars were still arriving behind her.

"What?" Michaud asked, watching her face.

"I have a gift for you."

"What gift?"

"Maurice."

"Maurice came to me willingly. He sees, now perhaps, the need to comply with my demands."

"He won't bring you the *tasse*, Raphael. The *tasse* is gone — dead when François died. Maurice doesn't have it."

I watched her profile. What was this? She knew François was in the wine cellar, where Raphael wouldn't go.

The commotion at the rear resolved. More black-shirted security — human, vampire, I couldn't tell — pushed through the crowd. Each one of the big men held someone who'd disobeyed the fine restaurant's dress code.

Anarchy Jim.

Stacy Grace.

Roland.

Watlin.

And Ian.

I closed my eyes, feeling an express elevator drop inside my chest. How had Leigh known? Unless, of course, she'd known all along.

Two extra guards came though the crowd, neither with a burden in tow. One held silver. The other held a pistol. I knew it wouldn't fire lead. In this den of the undead, protectors would fire wooden bullets.

I watched my friends struggle.

And I understood.

It didn't matter that I'd been able to feel François's energy, or sense his mind as if he was standing right beside me. Somehow, what Leigh said was true — hearing the words, here, let my mind *see* that it was true. François was as dead as he had every right to be. He *wasn't* in the wine cellar. I knew because as I reached back through the last bit of Ian's blood within me, the vision wavered. Yes, I saw an old man and yes, his vibes felt right. But the old man never showed his face. *In Ian's maker's blood memory, I never saw my old friend's face.*

That meant it was a fabricated memory. A trick of the mind. A decoy vision, planted by Leigh through methods unknown, to lure us here.

Anarchy Jim was looking at me with apology, full of regret instead of the anger he had every right to feel. "I'm sorry, Maurice," he said. "We looked at every bottle down there, and none were handwritten like your picture."

This made Michaud's gaze rise. His attention perked. His head cocked.

"*Handwritten?* My friend, you don't mean our old Chateau Lafite?"

I looked at Jim, then Michaud. As if I could stop either from saying the next thing.

Jim didn't answer, but the expression on his face did. Michaud started to laugh. But whereas he'd only been chuckling before, this was a big-throated laugh. The kind that brings the house down.

"You laugh," Stacy said, "but he'll find it. Maurice always gets what he wants in the end."

I was torn between being touched and being ashamed. I wasn't getting *anything* right now. They were already cuffing me in silver, putting that loathed leash back around my neck. Vampire law is complicated, as are the rituals governing subordinates and superiors. We could have fought at any time, but there would have been consequences — especially if Vampire Council Guards were on their way for a ceremony I was beginning to suspect we'd walked right into. This time, it'd be different with the Council. This time, there was evidence against me. Normally, vampires don't need to build cases against one another. But Leigh wasn't a vampire — and if she meant to cash in and become one, this "grand gesture" for her master would need to be airtight: Michaud's rival caught red-handed and dead to rights.

"But *mon chéri*," Michaud said, still chuckling, "no matter how determined you are and no matter where you search, you will *never* find that precious bottle of wine."

Jim understood. "He drank it," he said.

"But no," Raphael said, surprised. "You did not tell them, Maurice?"

They all looked at me.

"*We* drank it almost a hundred years ago," he went on. "Together."

TWENTY-SEVEN

DEFLECTION

The presence inside Annabel sat up straight, strong enough to contort her posture. It was like feeling an iron skeleton beneath your skin, sitting still so it didn't rip through.

Ask more, that presence seemed to say. Or, with its familiar lisp: *Askth more.*

The mind inside her own was curious enough to make Annabel curious. She understood all that Maurice had said, but was most interested in what he'd said about the archive. Despite the revelation about the wine (something she didn't think Maurice had originally meant to say, but either conscience or belief in therapy had changed his mind), she wanted very badly to know about François — about the human archive that, it seemed, was dead after all. How did that work? It'd held such promise. Not for 1985 — more for its applications today.

If he doesn't have the archive after all, said that internal presence, *this was a dead end.*

"Wait. So François *was* dead?"

Maurice stammered before answering. He'd said that last bit like a punchline, and he'd clearly expected that the wine revelation, not François, would be the first thing she asked about.

"Y-yeah. He was dead. I should have known. He'd have been nearly a hundred, and last I'd seen him, he was already old and in poor health."

More, said the voice inside Annabel — the voice that wanted so badly to know how vampires hid memories, and how to unlock a locked mind. It was her husband's voice, so curious about what might lie in Maurice's undead cortex ... and, she sensed, how those memories intermingled with her own precious blood.

But she didn't think of that now. The voice shoved it away. It needed to know. It needed to *understand.*

"Anyway ..." said Maurice.

"No, hang on." Annabel held up a pausing hand. Something wasn't right. She saw a logical miss inside her mind, trying to track it down. Maurice's eyes were avoiding hers: He'd said something wrong. He'd take it back if he could — if she'd forget what was bugging her, and what he was accidentally giving away.

Then she had it.

"When *did* you see François last?" she asked.

"Before I left France."

"But he was young then. You said the last time you saw him, he was old."

"I meant, 'He'd obviously have *been* old.'"

"That's not what you said. You said 'the last I'd seen him, he was *already* old.'"

"You know what I mean."

Pivot.

"Did you really drink that wine?"

Pause. "Yes."

"When?"

"Also before I left France."

"*When* before?"

"I don't know. Why the hell does it matter?"

He was getting agitated. Normally she'd back off to let the patient learn for himself. But this was different. She kept hearing that lisping voice inside her head, feeling urgency, missing two things it wanted more than life itself. One was on the edge of Maurice's deception. She was the only one who could push him on this, so push she must.

"You said the two of you fought over that bottle of wine. Stole it back and forth. Buried it in the ground to keep it from each other as if it meant everything in the world."

"Yeah. So?"

"Well, then what made you stop and drink it?"

"I guess we figured enjoying it was better than spending all that energy fighting."

"You *figured*, or that's actually what happened?"

No response.

"*Maurice?*"

"That's what happened," he said.

She pondered, watching Maurice turn off again, watching him again cross his arms. He was a strange man. He didn't need to be here. He didn't *want* to be here. No force on the planet could have kept him here if he'd wanted to leave. And yet he was basically pouting: angry at Annabel for plying him, yet unwilling to put the obvious end to it.

He and Michaud had drank the wine — his prize bottle, held in spite between two rivals. That wasn't something you did simply to see it done. Wine collectors saved even moderate bottles for special occasions. A bottle as fine as the 1787 Chateau Lafite would have merited a very special occasion indeed. You didn't drink a wine that old and delicate to erase a score. You drank it on the eve of something momentous — a celebration, or the best of well-wishes.

She knew without a doubt: When they'd drank the Lafite, they'd done it as friends.

"Help me help you, Maurice," Annabel said.

"That's genius. It belongs on a Hallmark card."

"I'm serious."

"I know you are. That's what makes it so funny." He stood. He went for the door, grabbed his backpack.

"You're leaving?"

"Yes."

"But we're not finished."

"Really? Look at the time. We were done hours ago."

"You haven't finished the story, Maurice."

He shrugged. "Isn't that something you shrinks do? Cut the patient off, then say, 'That's all our time for today?'"

"I've allowed time. Plenty of time for you."

"No. *That's all our time for today.*"

"Why are you doing this?" she asked.

"Why are *you* doing this?"

"I'm your doctor."

"What else are you?"

She stopped. The voice inside her retreated.

"What's that supposed to mean?"

"Do you text all your patients between sessions?"

Annabel was prepared to cut that one off at the knees, but stopped short. She *had* texted him. A lot. When it occurred to her, which it didn't always, she assumed her motivation was akin to an intellectual crush: She hadn't known vampires existed, and now she did. As a studious, curious person, she told herself all those texts had been about wanting to know more. But as an objective, logic-based person, there were times that she doubted even her own motivations. Her questions had been about his last story — a lot about Daisy, the second vampire Maurice had turned only to watch her die. Something about Daisy's story had especially intrigued her.

"Sometimes," she said.

"I see something in you," he said. "Something in your eyes. It bothers me."

"You're projecting. We've reached an uncomfortable place in your story, so instead of choosing to face the discomfort, you've decided to attack me instead."

His impulse had softened. He still seemed ready to walk out the door, but he was lingering, his body language less impetuous already. He took a step forward rather than back.

"It's not an attack. It's something I feel."

"Patients often feel bonded to their therapists. It's just about transference, natural after we've spent so much time delving deep into your innermost—"

"No," he said.

"No?"

Another step forward. Watching Annabel's eyes. The presence inside her — that alien voice, which she only occasionally found strange to find occupying her head — backed almost entirely away.

"Did you know your parents? Were they your natural parents?"

"That's awfully personal."

"Did you?"

Now she was the one who felt defensive. "Not that it's any of your business, but yes and yes."

"Would you permit me to sample your blood?"

"What? No!"

"I can make it quick. Painless. I still have the balm that—"

Time to be decisive. She didn't like the sideways way he was looking at her. How had he turned this around? He didn't seem to be using glamour, but if she'd learned anything from her exposure to vampires, it's that they were always kind of glamouring you a little. His manner was smooth and calming. Talking to Maurice, even without guile, was like slow hypnosis. No wonder she lost track of time.

"Sit down, Maurice," she barked.

"I just want to see if—"

"Sit down!"

He waited an extra half moment, then sat. Now he was the one who looked spellbound.

"It's understandable that you'd deflect like this," she said. "I touched a nerve for you, and you don't like it, so you're naturally inclined to push away and try to make all of this about me. It's totally normal. But you're more ... *persuasive* ... than my human clients, so it's important that you know what you're doing. I'm automatically going to be a little slower to notice it and slower to put a stop to it when you step over the line, so if we're going to keep working together, I'm going to need a commitment from you, as much as you're able to make it."

"Okay," he said.

"I need you to try and remember that you came to me because you recognized, to your credit, that you needed help. On at least some level, you respected my abilities as a therapist, and you confirmed it by scheduling a follow-up appointment and coming back."

"I totally respect your abilities," he said. Docile now.

Shame had done its job; she'd successfully turned "about her" into "about him" again.

"If that's true," Annabel said, "then I need you to trust that I know what I'm doing, and that my questions are always meant to help you. I will not always push you in comfortable directions, Maurice. That's not how this works. You will be uneasy in this room. That's how you heal. And, given your much-longer-than-normal life and the violence you've experienced, you have more healing to do than most. Does that all make sense? Can we agree on at least that much?"

"Of course," he said. He'd settled some: not just sitting now, but looking as if he might stay a while. When he'd first sat at her command, he'd looked like he might spring up at any second.

"Now. What you were just doing was, again, deflecting. You didn't like my questions, so your instinct was to turn things around on me. It's not actual anger. It's not actual suspicion. It's just the most convenient, most effective alternative your brain saw to doing what I was pushing you to do."

"You mean, to talk about my past."

"To talk about a *version* of your past that's contrary to the story you've been telling yourself, or prefer to tell yourself. We all tell ourselves stories, Maurice. We want to believe we're brave even if we aren't, or right when we were probably wrong."

He sighed. "Okay. Fine. I'll trust you." He laid back again, eyes on the ceiling.

"So," she said, feeling the presence inside her mind begin to return. "Tell me about the day you drank that bottle of wine."

It's 1892, 400 years exactly since Christopher Columbus landed in the New World. As Europeans, we had a problem with it. *New World this, New World that* ... even all those years ago, without the Internet or television or modern news, we still found ourselves hearing every bit of it. I'd never been to America, so it was easy to find it distasteful. To us, America seemed like an upstart. Just over a hundred years ago — a blink to someone as old as me — they'd thrown the world's economy into turmoil because they'd had a beef with England. How boring. I was used to tyranny back then, so America wanting freedom felt like spoiled children acting out. France had given them that big statue to put in their New York harbor — wasn't that enough? They had as much freedom as the rest of us, if by no other virtue than distance from the motherland. Mostly, we sipped cognac and smoked cigars like rich humans and rolled our eyes.

We weren't trying to be elitists. Really we weren't. Or rather: We were, but not as steeply as you'd think. Raphael and I, like anyone, simply were who we were at the time.

We had worldviews shaped by our circumstances, our upbringing, and our histories. And at that time, our circumstances had as their backdrop an upsurge in European pride that immediately threatened to be batted back by the young assholes overseas. *We* were the old world. *We* had been civilized for millennia. America, just a centuries earlier, had been a land of wilderness. And *they* dared to challenge *us*?

Exhibit: 1889, Paris, the *Exposition Universelle*. As its centerpiece, the Eiffel Tower. Nobody had seen anything like it before — not the exposition, not the Tower. It was the tallest structure in the world at the time, and incontrovertible proof that France was king of the planet. And yet here we were, just three years later, Raphael and me sitting around griping on the eve of what would, by most accounts, be considered our exposition's successor and superior: The Columbian Exposition, better known as the Chicago World Fair.

The Chicago Fair didn't open until 1893, but by 1892 the writing was already on the wall. Construction had been underway for a few years already, and despite initial (and, in 1892, *current*) doubts that the architects would complete the thing on time, I knew they would. It would be larger and grander than the Paris expo — and, it seemed, boast a structure even more fantastical than the achievements of Eiffel: the enormous Ferris wheel, capable of holding two thousand passengers at once. The fact that it wouldn't be as tall as our tower didn't matter. With its views and splendor, that first wheel would be the talk of the globe. The Fair itself had staggering scope: a beautiful white city full of brand-new, resplendent buildings criss-crossed with canals ridden by custom boats. Electric lighting provided by huge dynamos. Over six hundred acres of land, 65,000 exhibits, and a hundred thousand people, we later learned, waiting to enter Fair on opening day. By the time it finally closed six months later, it'd been visited by nearly 30 million people — and this at a time when the entire US population was only about 65 million.

Raphael found it offensive. I found it offensive. After decades of feuding, the unfounded moxie of the upstart Americans had brought us back together.

I told this story to Jess and the others (minus Stacy, who'd kicked a guy in the nuts and run, and Watlin, who she'd dragged off with her) while we were held prisoner in Raphael's dungeon. Which, owing to Raphael's un-vampirelike fear of dank underground places, was actually on the 12th floor of his office tower. And it wasn't really a dungeon — not a traditional one, anyway. Ian and I were in silver handcuffs able to hold us, but the handcuffs holding Roland and Jess were lined in fur. Anarchy Jim, who'd been one too many for the fur-lined handcuffs available, was strapped to a padded table beside a bunch of black leather crops and a gimp suit in a glass display case.

We were in Raphael's sex dungeon, decorated at the height of 1980s fashion and done in Miami Vice colors. There was a giant lava lamp to my side that was shaped like a cock, boiling red globs from its tip like the worst STD ever. You'd think that'd make my telling the story easier purely for humor reasons, but it didn't.

"So you weren't enemies," said Roland.

The others waited, wanting to hear the answer — all but Jess, who'd told the room her version of our face-off with Michaud and Leigh before I'd been given a chance. In that version, I hadn't just shared a bottle of wine with my supposed arch enemy (*the* bottle of wine I'd sent them into peril for, knowing it didn't exist), but had actually plotted all of this with him. The first accusation was founded. The second was not. I'd told them all, repeatedly, that I'd come to America reformed, sick of the bullshit and posturing in Europe. I really *was* a punk, decades before punk existed. I *did* hate the status-quo; I *did* distrust politicians and seek to rock the boat every chance I got; I didn't, in any way, want anything to do with the haughty rich. I even told them a brief version of my story with Daisy and the Vampire Mafia to garner sympathy — a strategy that didn't work at all.

I was frustrated by their anger, even though I understood it. I was the same Maurice I'd always been with them. I hadn't changed.

Although ... I had lied a lot.

"Raphael and I *were* enemies," I said. "It was just like I told you."

Several of them gave me a stare, then looked away. Security had brought us here, tied us up in what they must've known were often hilarious ways, then left us alone until Raphael could finish his evening/morning and come deal with us. It wasn't just my wrists bound in silver. They'd also put a silver collar on me, silver leggings, even some sort of silver-threaded shirt. I felt like King Kong: a beast subdued so others could gawk. All that was missing was a platform and a thousand flashing cameras.

I went on.

"You've got to understand. This, here—" I indicated our group with what strength remained, hoping they knew I meant life rather than the sex dungeon. "—was the first time I've allied myself with humans — with *only* humans. I've had human friends before, but there was always at least my wife, Celeste, as well. She insisted on *vampire* friends, *vampire* acquaintances. She's not prejudiced; she just knows that when you're as different from the norm as we are, you need others around who experience life as you do.

It's not that I ever truly *liked* Raphael, beyond those first few years. It's more that he was one of the only vampires around — hence one of the only people who understood me. He was like a bad habit. I couldn't ever really kick him, no matter how I tried."

"What's the World Fair have to do with any of this?" Roland asked.

"We decided that I'd go to the Chicago Fair as a representative of European Vampirekind," I told him. "There was nothing official, of course — just me and Raphael, drunk on blood and many bottles of inferior wine, deciding we'd undertake this mission to restore European pride. We'd already put our fighting past behind us, reconciled for one of a hundred brief times. It wouldn't last. It *didn't* last. But to seal the deal — to celebrate our impending victory over America and their too-big attitudes — we decided to crack open the bottle of Chateau Lafite. I remember what Raphael said: '*A bottle this fine should not be consumed with the lips and tongue. It must be consumed with all the soul, on the heels of a conquest.*' That's where we were: on the heels of what felt like conquest. What's more, we were very much in 'I love you, man' mode that night, and so the second reason we wanted to open the Lafite was to remove it as a bone of contention. We wanted to stop worrying who owned the bottle and who didn't. We decided to drink it together, then never have reason to fight again."

"Did it work?"

I laughed. Of course it hadn't worked. I went to the Fair, did my thing, met a monster, then returned most of a year later. When I came back to France, I learned all over again that Raphael was and had always been a colossal asshole. After that, we never reconciled again. He thought we did, but that was just me playing games. That was the part of the story I still didn't want to tell, and wouldn't if I could avoid it.

"No," I said. "We fought, same as always."

Jess was making non-subtle noises of irritation, clearly trying to draw my attention. I gave it to her. She'd earned that much.

"You sent us after a bottle of wine that didn't exist in order to prove something to a man who, as it turns out, *knew* it didn't exist. You said it'd hurt his pride enough that he'd stop bothering us. You said we could hold the bottle hostage to get him off our backs. You let us think we were going in to help ourselves, but that was bullshit, wasn't it? You only ever wanted to help yourself."

"I had to get us in here, Jess. I thought they had the vessel." I'd tried to explain the *tasse débordante* to them already, along with the danger of letting it fall into the wrong hands. I don't think I'd been very successful, maybe because I couldn't explain why I hadn't just told them in the first place. The real answer? The truth made me look like an asshole, like I looked right now.

The door at the opposite end of the sex dungeon opened. I readied myself for Raphael, but it was Leigh who entered.

"So the cellar was empty?" She turned her lips to a pout. "Such a pity. Such a surprise."

I said, "You planted the memory of François. He was never there."

She nodded. "It wasn't easy. The staged memory had to be prominent enough for you to stumble over when you sampled his blood—" Indicating the now-vampire Drag Worm Ian, restrained at my side. "—but not *so* prominent as to feel obvious."

"But ... how?"

"One of Raphael's men is in love with me. Adam. You met him that first night, when you broke into the nest? Tall, with a narrow face?"

I remembered. I'd seen him that night; I'd seen him twice more. No wonder he hadn't attacked when we'd invaded the nest. Even then, he was part of a plan.

"Raphael was Adam's maker, just like Adam is *his* maker." Again indicating Ian. "Between Raphael's complaining about the past and Adam's blood-ties connection to Raphael's mind, we got a pretty good idea what François looked like, how old he'd be today, and a few other details. Adam glamoured an old human, then 'experienced his presence' in a general, from-a-distance way that didn't show his face. Given the right context, I thought you might believe him to be François. It must have worked," she said, "because you sure came running."

"You turned Ian *specifically* so I'd find that memory inside him," I said.

Leigh nodded. "After a few brushes with Raphael, it'd be natural for you to go snooping. Adam told me some of Raphael's memories of you, too. He told me how impetuous you are for such an old man. You'd think nothing of blood rape to learn what you needed to know."

"Ian allowed it," I said.

"Well." She looked at Ian. "Then I guess Ian's a whore, too."

"I suppose that's how you knew we were coming here tonight? Because your flunky was spying on us through Ian's eyes?"

Leigh shrugged.

Jess said, "Jesus, Maurice. You didn't even make it hard for her."

"*You* try seeing someone else's memories, Jess. Let's see how you do."

"You don't get to be pissy with me right now," she said. "Believe me, that's the *last* thing you get to do."

I looked away, angry and feeling stupid. She'd led me like a donkey follows a carrot on a stick. Was I really that gullible? But no; it wasn't really as she'd described. When I'd watched that vision of "François" in the wine cellar, it'd been as much feeling as sight. Adam's memory, though new, had somehow put me back in time, walking through the cellars. Leigh hadn't shown me a movie. She'd given me a full-body immersion, all the way up to my brain and emotions.

"But ..." Talking to Leigh now, as if I could make the false memory true. "But I could *feel* François in your vampire's blood. When I was in that memory, it was like I was standing right beside him."

"You were."

I raised my head, met her eyes proper.

"*Un vin est aussi beau que son créateur,*" she said.

And I understood. All at once, I understood the depth of the shit I'd stepped in. As I did, Leigh gave a tiny smile and left the dungeon.

Anarchy Jim was looking around, fearful, trying to understand.

"What did she say?"

"A wine is only as beautiful as its creator," Roland translated, shocking us all.

They all looked at me. Jess said, "What the hell does that mean, Maurice?"

I swallowed.

"It means we're fucked," I told them.

TWENTY-NINE
LOCK AND KEY

I'm two thousand years old. I've fought hordes in wars, never minding when I got surrounded. I've been on trial for my life (sometimes as a demon and sometimes as a warlock, including two memorable times as a vampire) and always escaped, cool as a cucumber. I've been bound by my kind, pursued by humankind, chased away, and feared with red-hot terror. I've moved in and out of society, always hiding, always in the dark, always able to find a niche in which to stay despite the day and its prejudices. I survived European tumult, American expansion, and the advent of daytime talk shows. And yet I've seldom felt as trapped as I did that day in Raphael's dungeon.

Un vin est aussi beau que son créateur. A wine is only as beautiful as its creator.

Something François used to say. Only to me, never to Raphael — because whereas I appreciated wine, it was François's and my opinion that Raphael bulldozed his way through it. I loved learning the nuances of the many regions, flavors, makers, and vintages. I wanted to hear about the minerals in the soil, the way humidity and neighboring plants could alter the flavor of the grapes. As old as I was and as steeped as I'd previously felt I was in wine, I found I could always learn something new from François.

Raphael, on the other hand, drank and collected for status. The better wine he consumed, the more his ego was sated. So it was with *me* that François shared his knowledge — in that cellar, browsing the many beautiful bottles. It was with me that François shared that gem, about a wine being an expression of its maker's skill and passion.

I suppose François might have spoken his trademark line to someone else, and that it might have made its improbable way to Leigh so she could lay it on me now, when I was most vulnerable. Technically, that was possible. But given how I'd felt inside the false memory — that sense of familiarity, as if I was immersed rather than just seeing — the truth was something far more likely:

Somehow, even though it was a lost art from a bygone age, Leigh had learned the skills to become a *tasse débordante* — a human vessel — herself.

She'd found François, somehow.

Then she'd scooped all of our stored knowledge from inside him, either through persuasion or force. She'd taken it into herself, still locked, still mostly inaccessible — useless, since neither of them could open the archive and see what was inside. But if she'd really done that — if she'd become so much of what used to be François — it explained why the fake memory had persuaded me. I'd felt like François was in the memory with me because in a way, he had been. Only it hadn't been François, not really. It was Leigh's mind — the new *tasse* — that I'd felt.

She'd acquired François's mind. Now *she* was the vessel.

"Maybe you'd better explain," said Jess.

And I sighed. Yes, I'd better.

So I told them about the idea of a *tasse* again, for clarity. I told them how Raphael had amassed vast piles of manipulative information, including secrets and blackmail. I explained the damage all that snooped information would have caused if it'd been released, and why, therefore, he and I had split ownership of it. Giving two vampires keys to the vessel was a little like giving two soldiers keys to a missle silo. Raphael and I weren't both required to open François's mind in the way both soldiers had to agree to launch missiles, but we were each other's check-and-balance nonetheless. If I'd unlocked François, Raphael would have known. If he'd done it, I'd have known. For years we filled the archive and made our minds forget what we'd entered, so the information would reside in François and nowhere else. Occasionally we swapped blood to verify the absence of duplicate memories inside us, ensuring that the vault was the only complete record. It was a good system. It worked ... until François left France. Until somehow, years later, Leigh had found François and taken what she wanted. Maybe she'd even killed him. By now, it didn't matter.

"You can just ... *steal someone's memories?*" Roland asked.

"Only for humans. Only for vessels. There's a process. I don't know it." I shook my head, frustrated. "*Nobody* knows it. *Tasses débordante* were already out of favor by the time *we* started using François. The few vampires who knew we had a *tasse* laughed at us for being impossibly old fashioned. We might as well have been drawing on cave walls. The know-how of transferring a vessel into a new brain is even *more* old-fashioned, even *more* obscure. It's *so* obscure, all I really know is that it's technically possible. It's supposed to be incredibly difficult. And *pointless*. Humans can't unlock *tasse* archives. François couldn't see what we'd hidden inside him, and neither can Leigh. All she's done is to transfer a black box."

"So why are you worried, if she can't even open what's inside her head?"

It was a fair question. Michaud could open it, but the fact that Leigh didn't seem to have told him she had it suggested enlisting his help wasn't part of the plan.

That really only left one option, taking me right back to *We're fucked.*

"Vessels can't be read by human brains," I said. "*Human* brains. But if she becomes a vampire ..."

"Wouldn't she still need the key?" Jess asked.

"If Raphael is the one who turns her," I said, "the maker bond will *give* her his key."

"Maybe he won't turn her," said Anarchy Jim.

But he didn't understand, so I explained: Raphael *had* to turn Leigh after 25 years of service and one big act of tribute ... such as capturing her master's biggest rival.

"I don't know," Jim said. "Guy like that? He must have bigger rivals than you."

What Jim didn't know was that Raphael *didn't* have a bigger rival. There *was* no one he hated more — and that would only get worse when Leigh, who was starting to feel like this whole thing's mastermind, told him the truth.

In truth, François — our *tasse débordante* — hadn't crossed the ocean on his own to follow me.

He'd crossed *with* me, bunking two decks above the storage area where I slept in loose earth.

I'd paid for his ticket.

I'd persuaded him to go.

It was my fault the vessel had been in America for Leigh to find, copy, and dispose of.

Everything Raphael hated me for, Leigh somehow knew, was true.

THIRTY

PUPPETS

We'd been like puppets to her.

I realized it the longer I sat and thought, now an hour past Leigh's departure. She'd moved us here and there on invisible strings, possibly for a very long time. She'd uncovered my deepest secrets, exploiting them years before I knew she existed. She'd made us do whatever she wanted, as if we had no will of our own.

I wasn't sure of the specifics (I'd never had familiars, let alone kept one on the hook for a quarter century), but from context I gathered there was a ritual to Graduation. First Leigh needed to put in her 25 years, which she'd already done. Then, she'd need to formally petition the Vampire Council for Graduation, which she'd surely *also* already done. The big gesture for her master (in Leigh's case, capturing me and proving my guilt) struck me like a grad student's thesis: required as a final exam, subject peer review. Those peers would arrive as delegates from the Vampire Council. They'd hear Leigh's case, review her work, then require Michaud to turn her. I imagined the whole thing grossing him out, what with his germophobia.

He'd make them all wear gloves. He'd make them transfer the blood using a Belligrand, like a vampire poseur.

There was only one problem. Considering the way Leigh *had* moved us around like puppets, I doubted Graduation would be the end of her scheming. Once she was turned, she'd be able to unlock the *tasse* archive inside her head by using the key in Michaud's blood ... and when she did, Michaud would feel it. He wouldn't like that — not at all. He'd consider it a betrayal, worthy of punishment. And he wouldn't even *have* to wait that long, because *I'd* tell him the truth when I saw him. That all meant two things: One, Leigh couldn't let Michaud live, lest he destroy her. She'd have to kill him, or scheme to have him killed, before opening the archive. And two, she couldn't let me blab before Graduation. I had to survive through Graduation because I was evidence, so she'd keep us separate until it was over, then dispose of me — of all of us. But she couldn't keep Michaud away from me for very long, could she? He'd be eager to see me, eager to talk. And that meant Graduation would need to happen as soon as possible. Tonight. *Immediately.* It might even be happening now ... and afterward it wouldn't just be us who was fucked. Michaud would be a dead man walking, waiting for a knife in the back. Or a wooden stake.

That was bad. But if possible, the doubt Leigh's scheming had cast on what I'd assumed were my own choices was worse.

Everything I'd done and everywhere I'd gone, I now suspected Leigh of orchestrating.

I'd rambled before coming to Austin, but now I wondered: Had I *really* rambled? I'd followed my gut, which for a vampire is mingled with blood. Just as anyone is susceptible to subconscious hints, vampires are susceptible to blood suggestions. Leigh had Ian's maker wrapped around her finger, so it stood to reason she may have enlisted the help of others. Vampires a small world. If you look deeply enough, everyone is related to everyone. She'd fooled me with a fake memory of an old man, so why couldn't she have fooled my blood in other ways? I'd thought I was free. I thought I'd made my own decisions. But what if I hadn't?

With the others now refusing to talk to me — especially after confessing to stealing François as Michaud had accused — I sank into my blood's miasma. I let the thoughts and memories swirl — not just my own, but those of my maker and kin. I saw coincidence after coincidence, wondering now if any had truly been coincidental.

Puppets, all of us. Including Michaud.

I'd come to Austin without knowing Michaud was here, and Michaud had settled on Austin for his development company without knowing I might someday come to the same city. For years we'd lived in the same basic place, always shielded from one another until the appropriate time: until Leigh's 25 year anniversary, at which point the act of capturing me stopped being a neat favor and became *the act* that ushered Leigh into vampirekind. She'd known about François: known about our connection and the fact that I'd stolen him (an idea she'd managed to foster inside of Raphael, fanning the flames), known he was here because of me, knew how I'd react if I found out he was still alive. The tapestry Leigh wove would have fallen apart without a thousand tiny tweaks — a task she must have handled as deftly as any project manager. Things had to unfold just right for her plan to come to fruition. Somehow, I knew from logic and the fog of blood memory, she'd architected every detail.

Michaud, as one piece on a chessboard.

Me, as another.

At some point in the past, there'd been François as well. François, who'd been old when Leigh was young, who she'd found only after I'd lost touch with him, without either of us knowing. There'd been whoever had taught her vampire law, whoever had taught her how to become a vessel, whoever had shown her the obscure archives to seek out in order to learn the tricky task of moving one vessel's contents into a new host. With François's knowledge, she'd taken bits of François himself — bits she revealed to me only when she needed to bait me. Bits she'd managed to keep from Michaud.

She'd been at this for *years*.

"I just can't believe this, dude," said Anarchy Jim. Hearing his disappointment broke my heart. He'd always been so trusting, so enthusiastic. I'd taken that trust and enthusiasm and bent it to my will. I was no better than Michaud, or Leigh. No better than politics or the presidency.

"I was looking out for all of us," I said.

"Fuck you, dude," he said, snapping in an instant. "Like Jess said, you were looking out for yourself."

"Hey. If anyone has any ideas, I'm all ears," I said. But we'd been over this and over it. Leigh hadn't planned this well to leave anything to chance.

"Be a vampire," said Jess. "You got us into this. You get us out."

"I can't do anything in all this silver."

"Then pick the lock. Fly. Become fog. Whatever the shit you're supposed to be able to do."

Now she was just being spiteful. She'd had a vampire mother. She knew what I could do and what I couldn't.

I looked away. We'd been circling bad ideas for hour. The others expected a miracle, but vampires had limits. Leigh had lured me to the building in daylight for a reason. Living alongside vampires for so long had taught her our weaknesses.

"Pick *your* lock, if you're so smart," I said.

"Don't get bitchy with me," Jess snapped. "You don't get to act superior right now."

"Maybe later?"

"You're so funny. You're *so goddamn funny*, Maurice."

"What do you want from me? I made a mistake!"

"What do I *want*? Okay. Here's what I want. I *want* you to go back in time and tell the motherfucking *truth!*"

"I told you all I could."

"Fuck you! I wouldn't even know you were a vampire if I hadn't forced it out of you! Is your name even Maurice?"

"Of course it is."

"*Of course.*" She mimicked my tone. "Oh yes. *Of course.* How could I doubt you? It's not like you're the exact opposite of everything you said or anything."

"What's that supposed to mean?"

"What do you think? You aren't one of us. You *are* the establishment. You *are* control. You *are* rules and privilege and everything this group is supposed to stand against."

"That's not true."

"You won't even admit it!" She was so exasperated, it was over the top. "Jesus Christ, Maurice ... I could maybe have an ounce of respect of you if you'd just own what you did, or what you are. Just own *one thing*. But when have you copped to *anything* that made you look less than awesome?"

I looked away, shaking my head.

"Clamming up, I see," she said.

"What the hell do you want me to say, Jess?"

"Say you've got a plan! Say you'll get us out of here! Say you've got an ace up your sleeve, because maybe once, *just for a goddamn second*, you chose to do something that wasn't just selfish! Say that for at least *one motherfucking second*, you decided to put someone's needs ahead of your own!"

But with that, she had me. I never really thought of them, never really had. The only selfless gesture I had left, ironically, would be to admit how shitty I'd become.

"You want me to say it?" I blurted. "Fine. *Fine!* Yes, I was just like Raphael. We were two peas in a pod. He was a scheming, manipulative, bourgeoise asshole and *I* was a scheming, manipulative, bourgeoise asshole. We wanted to build an empire, just for us. When I came to America the first time, it was to plant seeds. Never mind that I *stopped a fucking murderer* in the meantime."

"What are you talking about?"

"My *grand plan*," I said, bitter enough to be sarcastic. "I only do things that benefit me, right? Chicago? For me. Coming back to America? For me." The sarcasm broke. "Wake up, Jess. *Everyone* is selfish. At least in my life, I've had thousands of years to mix it up. The truth is, you *don't* know me. I went through a phase, is all, just like all of you are going through a phase. The only difference is, my asshole phase feels long to you because it lasted a human lifetime. You don't believe I am who I say I am — that I'm a better person today? Well *fuck you*, Jess! I didn't keep secrets to manipulate you. I did it because I hate the vampire I was back then more than you possibly can. I was embarrassed, okay? Stealing François from Michaud was the only thing close to selfless I did back then, but who am I kidding? I originally stole François so I could use him, not free him. Only after we were all the way across the fucking ocean did the truth strike me — did *my wife's better sense* strike me — and I let him go. I can't erase any of that. I'm just trying to do what I can right now, but I can't change the past. So go ahead. You want to shit on me? Bring it on. I'm too busy shitting all over myself to care."

I crossed my arms as best I could, but the handcuffs were in the way.

Jess said, "So is that your apology?"

"What the hell do you think?"

"I think it's self pity. Even now, you can't help making this all about you."

"Yeah, man," said Drag Worm Ian. "This is my first time being able to feel other people's emotions inside me, and I'm still less of a cock than you."

Something about that made my brow furrow. Ian, showing empathy. Ian, connecting to others through his blood. An idea was on the tip of my tongue, or perhaps the tip of my mind. A way out, a way *through*. What was I missing?

The door rattled. Then someone outside, angry, began to kick. It must have locked by mistake. Leigh was back, with enforcers in tow, maybe to lay her claim before Michaud could hear what we had to say. Maybe with a wooden stake. Maybe to kill us.

But it wasn't Leigh who finally crashed through the door. It was Watlin, with Stacy Grace behind him.

"We found some Ho-Ho's in a kitchen down the hall," Watlin said, coming forward with what looked like a hack-saw. "Let's roll, bitches!"

Even after pulling Jess and Ian aside to discuss the idea I'd had, Jess still wouldn't talk to me. Roland and Jim had at least moved to neutral despite being excluded, but Jess remained an asshole.

"Do you hear what I'm saying?" I asked her for the third time.

"The problem is that I've heard what you're saying every time before. And look where it's gotten me?"

"This is hardly the time for—"

"Sorry," she cut me off. "Out of breath."

And so she sounded, maybe a little, as we ran down the hall behind Watlin and Stacy. Jess struck me as winded but not impossibly so — more refusing to talk out of spite than anything legit.

I ran on, not winded at all, letting Jess have her way.

The hallways were deserted. Maybe that made sense; maybe this was where the vampires, mostly sleeping now, kept their offices. Maybe that's why there'd been nobody outside the dungeon's door, nobody in the hallway, nobody at the stairwell or elevator. There were no obvious security cameras. Was that for discretion? Or something else? I couldn't shake the same feeling I'd had before: that our path was just a little too clear. I thought of convenience. I thought of coincidence. *How lucky*, I thought, *that they locked the door but left us otherwise unguarded. And how fortunate, in turn, that our two friends escaped and were able to find us without problem.* How had they even known where we were? It was all so serendipitous.

"You okay, Maurice?" That was Stacy, who hadn't heard the whole story and didn't know how much she should hate me.

"I'm fine."

"Is Jess okay?"

"She's better than me."

Jess's head ticked. She'd heard me, but I hadn't meant it as a compliment. It was a jab, meant to get her talking. It failed. We ran on, the entire building's length, toward the staircase.

"Elevator, bitch!" said Watlin, excited for some reason.

But I grabbed his finger before he could press the button. We needed stealth, and stealth wasn't an elevator ascending to a vacant floor. I dragged him with us, finally light with my silver burdens removed, weakened now only by the knowledge that outside, the sun was bright and hot. We'd have to find a way out somehow, but I doubted we'd be as lucky in the loading dock as we'd been so far.

We'd find a way. Somehow. We opened the stairwell door instead.

Two minutes later and two floors down, another door opened. A man in a long white coat entered, noticing us once fully inside. He was human. Normally, I wouldn't have been able to tell with the other humans around me, but adrenaline had me amped up to ten. Despite my fatigue, I felt I could punch through walls. Just as, even from here, I could smell the man's fear, and know it for human fear. He'd had that fear the moment he entered — before he'd looked up to see us charging down. Whatever had scared him, it was beyond that door, on that lower floor. I could even smell the *breed* of his fear: not mortal fear, and not worry. This was the kind of fear that comes with awe, as if for a greater power. It was the fear I used to smell on ancient people, before they understood the movement of planets, when they witnessed an eclipse.

It was enough, almost, to stop me.

It did stop Ian, Watlin, and Jess. They looked at the man; he looked at them. He had a pack over one shoulder and a handful of burdens.

When he saw me, his old fear tinged with new fear. I was sure he recognized us somehow, maybe knew what our descent meant. He was a man who'd walked in on something private — something not just embarrassing, but dangerous as well — now scrambling to escape.

He retreated, back to the floor from which he'd come. The door began to close. Jess's shoulders relaxed, her ribcage collapsing. She'd been holding her breath, assuming we were caught. Seeing the man — seeing what he carried — I felt the exact opposite. Instead of running from him, I ran toward him, panic threatening.

I shoved past, muscles twitching. Vampires have the prickling instinct of wolves. Mine, after seeing the man, had pressed a cold finger against my spine.

"Maurice!"

Jess, suddenly concerned. I looked back, saw her expression shift back to accusatory, knew she wasn't sure how to feel about me. But we'd both seen what was beyond that door, and she knew I was going for it in pursuit of the

fleeing human: bright sunlight from unblocked windows —
a vampire killing ground..

I flinched, but she grabbed me.

"Don't."

"That man was holding a Belligrand."

"A *what?*" said Ian.

But of course he didn't know. His turning had been the
raw type: teeth on skin. But I'd been right about Michaud:
He didn't want to bite or be bitten. He preferred his blood
transfers the cold, quasi-medical way. Just like the transfer
that was underway now, or already over.

There was half a beat. No more than a few millisec-
onds, just long enough for Jess and I to make sure each other
understood. Her eyes told me not to go — not even as
furious with me as she was.

But I'd seen that device. The Belligrand. With my
vampire eyes, I'd seen it magnified, in high-definition,
frozen in time. Its tip was wet. Already red. It'd been used,
quite recently.

I gave chase, blurred to superhuman speed. I paused at
the door, but only for as long as it took to scope for danger.
The hallway, from my new vantage, was pocked with long
rectangles of bright sunlight, broadcast through the office
doors opposite. My hesitation and Jess's protests had taken
only a few seconds, and the man was still visible just a
handful of offices down, running, glancing back as I took my
second to regroup.

Then I dashed. Through the first beam of light, feeling
my skin blister instantly. I stopped in the shade, recovering
too slowly, feeling the seconds tick away. Even the areas
without sunbeams were insufferable. The white walls
reflected radiation into the ambient space. Even motes of
dust caught the sunlight and warmed my skin. I counted to

three, faster than a human would count to one, and dashed again. Stopped. Counted. Dashed.

To the man I was chasing, my progress must have looked like stop-motion — like one of those hideous Japanese horror flicks. I'm blindingly fast when I want to be, so even stopping to heal between sunbeams I caught up with him easy. I tackled him, knocking his backpack away, spilling his armload of goods. I saw that what I'd taken for a coat was actually a doctor's cloak, white enough in the reflected sunlight to hurt my eyes.

I had my hands on his throat, eyes scanning the detritus, by the time Jess and Watlin caught up with me. Ian was still in the doorway. He wouldn't brave the sun as stupidly as I had.

Jess saw my look. Wordlessly, she lowered my ire. I breathed more deeply but refused to let go of the doctor's collar. Then Jess's eyes went to my left hand and she gasped. It was just moving from black to an ugly, boiling red but refused to heal further in this whitewash. My face must have looked the same on the sunlight side. She looked at it now, reaching out, seeming to want to touch. To help, if she could, despite how furious she'd recently been.

"Your skin ..."

"It's fine. It'll heal." I tightened my grip on the doctor, who'd rather ill-advisedly tried to worm out of a two-millennium-old vampire's grip. He was human all right, and probably inches from pissing his pants. I said, "Where is she?"

"Who?"

"Leigh Everness!"

"I don't know what you're talking about."

I raised my burnt fist, then drove it into the floor a half-inch from his face. There was concrete beneath the flooring. My fist went through the wood, an inch into stone. Chips flew, dusting his face. He screamed and flinched, hands rising to protect his eyes.

"*Leigh Everness.*"

"I ... I ..."

"An easier one, then. Raphael Michaud."

His eyes ticked toward the length of hallway. Not where he'd been running, but the other end.

Jess was tugging at me. For her, this wasn't a mission. There was no right or wrong here — not anymore. For the others, this was now a matter of escape. They'd come to steal wine, and even if they'd found the old Frenchman I'd hoped they'd find instead, it still would have been done for liberty. My friends weren't warriors. All they'd wanted was to save their shithole punk club. With that irrelevant as we ran for our lives, I was the only one interested in stopping to chat.

But *fuck you, Jess.* Her words were in my ears, loud and refusing to stop:

Say that for at least one motherfucking second, you decided to put someone's needs ahead of your own for a change!

This time, I wasn't just going to walk away.

"Maurice! We have to go!"

"Go. Run. I'll handle things here."

I know how I must have sounded. People say I'm intense, especially when I feel I've got something to prove. Still Jess tugged at me, now as afraid for me as angry at me. Afraid for all of us. The hallway was an ultraviolet death zone. Most of the building would be this time of day, no matter where I went. As to the rest of them? Well, if we were in the middle of a vampire power play, I think we all doubted a few humans had a chance to survive.

"Someone's going to see us!"

I had my doubts. There's a feeling that buildings get when they're empty, and it's not just an absence of activity. Jess was right; it was mid-morning on a weekday and the building should have been teeming with workers. Not all of Fleur-de-Lis's business involved biting; there were towers to build and parcels of land to acquire. So where were all the people? Floor after floor of workers had taken the day off. Office after office stood empty.

I knew a ritual's privacy when I saw it. She'd given everyone the day off, having already scheduled Graduation.

I scoured my mind for knowledge about Belligrand turnings. To me they were freak shows: the doctors in masks and latex gloves, the gleaming metal of the sterilized device. I looked at it now, near my shaking prey's right hand, probably on its way for cleaning because I could still see blood on it: Leigh's blood, Michaud's blood, possibly both mingled together. I didn't know enough to have a clue how long it took to turn a human that way or what the procedure determined for after. Where were they? Just like the ritualized clearing of the building, there were rules, policies, and procedures to obey for a Graduation. She'd be somewhere for formal recovery: not quite vampire, no longer quite human. It was information I didn't have, and that I'd need to find elsewhere if this sap beneath me didn't start talking.

I hit him in the face, impatient enough to turn merciless.

"*Where are they?*" I roared at him. "*Where are Leigh and Raphael!*"

I could see him trying to respond, too terrified to do so. It was hard to blame him. The procedure had probably been frightful. Raphael hated turnings. The idea of someone drinking his blood was disgusting to him. The notion of imbuing progeny with vampire power, I knew, seemed to him to be a diminishment of his own. He'd never made progeny, so far as I knew. If Leigh's politicking had forced his hand, I knew he'd be in a foul mood — especially since, if she had already been turned, the quickness of it would mean she'd already had everything lined up: permits applied-for, paperwork signed, witnesses present, doctors hired, approval recorded and granted the second Michaud verified my capture and Leigh's proof of what I'd done. That, I'd decided while Jess was shunning me, had probably been the magic ingredient: *proof.* At any time, Michaud could have come for me himself. If Leigh's capture of his biggest rival was to have meaning, the Council would want proof that I was, indeed, her maker's enemy. To get her turning approved, she'd have told the Council all she knew about me and Michaud, me and François. I'd be in trouble with them again ... but how was *that* new?

The doctor stammered. I heard feet approaching. The concrete building, empty as it was, confused my ability to echolocate. I could have readied for battle from whichever direction it came, but I didn't want a fight; I wanted to find my quarry in stealth. This was no longer about a safe exit. I wanted Jess and the others gone to safety, but for me, I had a wrong to right.

"Maurice!" Jess was dragging me now, and still the mute asshole on the floor couldn't find his tongue.

"Ian!" I hissed.

He looked up.

"Catch!"

I picked up the doctor, then threw him the length of the hallway. Ian caught him — pretty coordinated for a vampire so young. On my nod, Ian dragged the man back to the stairwell. I applied my rear to the wall opposite the sunbeams, pressed hard, and crashed through into the office beyond. I was breaking perpendicular walls and hauling ass for the stairwell a fractional second later under new cover: one more wall between me and the sun. It was faster than start-stopping, if more destructive. As long as none of the walls I crashed through was load-bearing, it'd be okay.

I came through the final wall near the elevator, then followed them into the stairwell. The whole thing took no more than two seconds.

"*D-down*," said the doctor when I turned to him, my glare asking the same old question. Being thrown and seeing me run through walls must have freed his tongue.

"You were up on this floor. If they're downstairs, why were you—?"

"A-autoclave."

I wanted to roll my eyes. This was a real estate company. Why did it have an autoclave? But I knew the answer: Raphael's germaphobia all over again. He couldn't just be a bloodsucker, could he? No, he had to have his meals extracted from donors with a syringe. He employed doctors, he had equipment sterilized after using. Of course he'd have an autoclave to sterilize the needed equipment ... but if so, why had the doc been exiting the floor with everything still dirty?

Time for that later. Right now, I had to find Leigh and Raphael.

"*What floor?*" I demanded.

"Four!"

We started walking, something still bugging me. Halfway down the next flight, the door behind us jolted as if it was going to open, then didn't. Someone was arriving at it — maybe those tromping feet I'd heard. But if there was someone there, they didn't seem interested in rushing into the stairwell. It was almost as if, they'd blocked us in.

There was a similar crash from the floor below us: blocked in all over again.

I grabbed the doctor, pulled him close, then ripped his collar back to reveal his neck. There were two scabbed-over puncture wounds above his carotid artery.

"He's a familiar," I said. "He's working for someone."

Maybe not even a doctor. Maybe just someone sent to lure us—

There was a much larger clang — this time of a door opening — from below. Bodies entered, but this time I smelled no humans. This time, I smelled no fear.

—to lure us where they wanted us to go.

A second door opened from above. Leigh entered, surrounded by black-clad soldiers. There were soldiers below, too. I recognized the uniform. They were Vampire Council Guard, sent by the ruling body to bear formal witness and protection for Leigh's Graduation.

"It's a trap," said Watlin.

We all looked at him. He grinned, despite our situation.

"I've just always wanted to say that," he added.

THIRTY-TWO
FIGHT

You saw this coming, I reminded myself as my breath came faster.

It was easier to think than to feel comforted by. The stairwell seemed too tight, my companions too fleshy and fragile. We'd been flanked from above, anticipated from below. Had we even escaped the dungeon, or had we been *allowed* to leave? Had Watlin and Stacy gotten lucky in finding us, or had they been led?

I looked up. Saw four Guard, collars up, masks on. Behind them, Leigh looked both strong and fragile. I could tell she'd been turned already, just minutes ago. This young and with her transformation incomplete, even Ian could have caught her and snapped her neck. But still there was something new and glowing about her: a clarity of skin, a brightness in the eyes, a sheen to her hair that I didn't think had been there before. Vampirism locks a person into wherever they physically are, but it brings out the best in them first. Vampire blood had made her radiant. Looking at her now, there was no question who was in charge — or who very soon would be.

Footsteps on the concrete stairs below us. I turned my head, trying to ignore Jess's shivering. Watlin was still Watlin: more excited about the forthcoming spectacle than the probability of his own death. Ian, I think, wasn't sure *how* to feel. On one hand, context must have told him he couldn't fight these soldiers — but on the other hand, he hadn't been challenged since turning. His fangs were down. His eyes were bright. If he fought, he'd probably die. Right now, he didn't care.

I focused on the footsteps, leaning over the railing catch a better look. I saw Raphael marching toward us, still in his work shirt, still in red suspenders. His hair was perfect and gelled. His right sleeve was uncharacteristically rolled above the elbow — perhaps for the donation owed to Leigh, by law, on the Council's orders.

Raphael looked up. We exchanged a glance. Knowing what I knew, I wished it were just the two of us here, *mano a mano*. We didn't share blood ties so we couldn't hear each other's thoughts, and it's not like I could shout to him what I wanted to say and what I wanted to make sure he knew — the one thing we might have mutually agreed on. The Guard, present by law at Graduations, only added bodies to the count. I'm usually pretty confident, but not in daytime, not against eight strong peers. I'd heard the Council Guard trained for daylight combat, often in cumbersome darksuits.

They marched up from below and down from above. Leigh waited, a tiny smile on her wide lips, her look seeming to say, *I got you.* Then Michaud, below, his glance telling me something entirely different.

I held my nerve. I walked down, gripping the railing. There were two floors between us. I kept losing sight of Michaud as I went down and he went up due to the turns, but as we neared, I looked right into his soul.

"You stole from me," Michaud said.

"Did I?"

"Leigh knew. She hired detectives. She scoured records."

"It's almost as if she had someone spying on you, to even know the *tasse* existed for me to steal."

He ignored my accusation. He said: "She has proof."

My eyes flicked up. Met Jess's eyes. I heard her criticism. I heard her hate, inside my head.

Even now, you can't help making this all about you.

I bit back denial. Yes, I *had* stolen from him. I *had* told François a better life awaited us in America, and then under cover of night we'd slipped away, boarding that steamship for the New World. Celeste hadn't known until I showed up with François and the passenger ticket I'd purchased in advance. Celeste and I didn't need tickets. We were cargo. I had such fine plans, that day. I wanted to build my own empire, heavy with ill-gotten secrets and an unfair advantage. Later, it wasn't my own choice to surrender those plans. Celeste had convinced me. Only after enough badgering had I set François free.

It really *had* been about me, always and forever. Until it wasn't, like how it wasn't now.

Protest. Tell Michaud the truth. Tell the Guard. But there was no point. Even if they'd believed me — even if they'd thought I wasn't just ratting out anyone I could to save my skin — I still refused on principle. I knew how this had to happen. I couldn't try talk my way out of it. I had to take it on the chin, owning my failure. *Through,* went the expression, *is the only way out.*

"I'm not denying it," I told Raphael.

"Then make amends for it."

I looked up and down. The Guard below had stayed

behind. He must have told them he'd handle me alone, which was something anyone who knew Michaud would have predicted: me, his henchmen, Leigh, even my friends, based on the stories I'd told. Pride was everything to Raphael. That was why my wine ploy, had it been real, would have done the job of forcing his hand.

Above me, the Guard were descending. Seeing this, I flexed to go back up to protect Jess, Ian, and Watlin, but Michaud beat me to it. Just as he'd urged the Guard below to stay in place, so too did he wave at the Guard above. They stopped, then retreated and began to wait. I knew the rules of our world; I knew they'd been sent as witnesses as much as soldiers. What was about to play out would be one on one: me against Raphael. But even if I killed him and won, there was no point. They'd grab me. I'd be too weak and too singular to resist. Even if I survived this battle, I was dead in the end.

There was no way out for me. No way but to die.

"You can't win, Maurice," he said. "If you strike me down—"

I squinted, then interrupted. "Are you ... Are you doing Obi-Wan Kenobe?"

He flushed. "No."

"Then tell me. What will happen if I strike you down? Will you become more powerful than I can possibly imagine?"

"Never mind."

"Or will I get a cookie if I strike you down? Because that sounds way better."

His face grew stern. He'd always had a shitty sense of humor.

"Although I guess that'd be winning," I said. "Maybe the cookie has coconut in it. You know how I hate coconut.

Maybe that's it. 'If I strike you down, I will get a cookie *filled with motherfucking coconut.*' Like a wish from a monkey's paw."

Raphael's eyebrows bunched. His mouth twisted into something sour. He was still dressed in that high-octane wardrobe of his: tie tight, little gold clip near the top. I had him bested, wearing my tuxedo. Looking back, it was a fight between James Bond and Michael Milken.

"Go on, Raphael," I said. "Throw me through the wall."

He came at me swinging. It was a big, showy hook rather than a more sensible jab, and even at vampire speeds I found him easy to dodge. My back went to the stone wall. I shot right, he hit to my left, breaking the concrete and his fist at the same time.

He pulled his hand back bloody. It was a stump of tangled used-to-be digits, smashed hard enough that two were halfway off. His mangled fist was covered in so much blood, he looked like Mola Ram fresh from ripping out a heart.

I didn't retaliate. Together we watched his fist heal and Raphael said of the blood, "These were my best French cuffs."

"It's okay. French cuffs are tacky."

He swung again. Shattered concrete behind me again.

"But at least you have shitty cufflinks to go with them."

Another swing. Now both sleeves were covered in gore. He'd lost a finger by now; it turned to dust below us like a carbon snake on the Fourth of July. Or perhaps Bastille Day.

"Come on, Raphael! Maybe I'm the one who should say that *you* can't win?"

Tired of punches and my wise-assery, he simply closed the distance, taking me in a full-body tackle. I tried to dart away again but he'd come with too much force, presumably a little agitated by my action-hero banter. He caught me easily, slamming hard into the wall. There was a puff of stone as my skull and back met cement hard enough to leave a Maurice-shaped indent. Gray dust showered my feet; a plop of what might be brain went with it. I felt wetness slough down my back, but I was temporarily too stupid to register its meaning. Until my brain healed, I was an idiot. He hit me again and again, bloodying my lip, bloodying my jaw, breaking my ribs.

Jess screamed above me. Ian shrank back, seeming to think that he was a vampire and maybe he should intervene. Roland, Stacy, and Jim were compressed into a knot, being as small as possible. Watlin, I saw through my brain fog, was eating a Ho-Ho.

I wanted to tell them that it was okay. I healed from just about anything, painful though it might be. But I didn't say that — partly because my speech centers were handicapped by concussion, partly because it'd only be temporarily true. One way or another, this was meant to be an execution. If I understood the law, the Council couldn't grant Leigh's Graduation without acknowledging its prerequisites: namely, that she had done her master a great service. In order for that service to be valid, I must be guilty on the evidence provided. They wouldn't reverse their decision now that Leigh had graduated, because doing so would admit the Council was fallible — and the Council, I knew, *never* admitted it was wrong.

They wouldn't let me leave the stairwell, whether it was Michaud who ended me or one of the Guard.

So I said nothing to Jess. I didn't tell her I was fine and I didn't promise it'd be okay. I couldn't beat them all — not with five humans and a baby vampire for my opponents to take hostage. I felt far from well, my head smashed, pain firing, my limbs broken as Michaud kept smashing my head to keep me stupid, then breaking all he could reach. This wasn't even the big finish; vampires don't usually hit to kill, because we can't be beaten to death. If Raphael was beating me now — and he most certainly was — it was payback for the humiliation I'd caused him. For making him look as dumb to the world as I felt with my brain leaking from my ears. This was his retribution, his saving-face. He'd abuse me and I'd take it, because it was my time, my duty, my only solution.

"*Fight back!*" he shouted at me. In his rage, his accent came out in full bloom. People think French is a lovely language, but when it's used in anger, it can be frightful.

He let my brain heal enough to comprehend, then repeated what he'd said. I didn't hesitate. He wanted to feel he'd earned his victory? Okay. I hit him through the chest hard enough to punch the railing behind him, bending it. On the way back out of his chest cavity, I grabbed his lumbar spine. You can't actually pull a spine all the way out. Mortal Kombat, years later, lied to us about that one. The long chain of bone always gets stuck on things inside — things like ribs, muscle, and intestine. You try to yank a spine, you get a daisy chain of gore like gutting a fish.

Michaud collapsed, unsupported, then twitched on the ground as he healed.

"Good enough?" I asked.

He grabbed my leg, twisted hard. My femur cracked in a spiral, unfurling like the twist in a Cinnabon. I knew because the jagged end erupted through my skin.

I elbowed him in the face, cracking teeth and nose. He came up like a fright mask with blood down his pressed collar and hit me with both arms, into the wall again in the same spot. This time the mortar turned to dust and the cinder blocks shifted. One tipped on its edge, teetering. Behind us must have been the elevator shaft, gory surprises at its bottom.

I ripped off a railing, impaled him through the neck. The effect was comical; he couldn't turn around without banging the walls. He broke it off and stabbed me right back through the shoulder. I swung, he dodged; we danced around and I bashed him against the same failing wall. More blocks shattered, falling into the elevator shaft like rain. We circled again: pugilists on the prowl. He swung at me, missed, punched brick. Through the wall's hole I could hear the elevator's motor, see the metal of the shaft's wall. One more swing and Raphael punched through that metal, tipping more of the cinder blocks in a dance toward the bottom.

I pushed back. We collided with a fire box: glass fronted with an axe inside. My back smashed it. I grabbed the axe from the shards. Jess inhaled a sharp gasp, probably anticipating *The Shining*. She didn't need to worry. I snapped the handle rather than swinging the head and, at the first opportunity, shoved it through Raphael's heart.

He stopped. Looked up at me. Gurgled blood. Above us, Leigh Everness made a noise.

Then Michaud said, "It's a *fiberglass* handle, asshole."

He tried to yank the handle out and found it stuck on his ribs. When I pushed him again, the collision between his back and the cinderblocks shoved the handle back out. He grabbed it and threw it away.

Then he shouted: "A little help?" I could tell it pained him to call for it, but I was too strong for him to beat alone. So far I'd been playing: matching him ounce for ounce, not truly going for the kill until the axe handle, which hadn't even been made of wood. Apparently I'd have to do better. I doubted I was getting out alive, but at least I could take Michaud with me.

The "help" he'd called for turned out to be an 18-inch wooden stake, tossed down from one of the Guard above: standard issue, probably, to wear on their Batman utility belts.

"Hang on," I said. "Maybe we can—"

He slammed the wooden stake into my chest. I felt it pierce everything, my breath short as my lung collapsed.

So this is what dying feels like.

He came at me once more, jamming the stake deeper. It was that first tackle all over again — but this time when I hit the wall, it crumbled behind me.

I fell. To the bottom of the elevator shaft. I didn't even feel the fire when it consumed me.

THIRTY-THREE

BASEMENT

I opened my eyes. I saw Jess above me. She slapped me and said, "Maurice! Maurice!" She slapped me again and again and again.

"I'm fine," I said, coming around.

"Maurice! Maurice!" More slaps, harder this time.

"I SAID I'M FINE."

"I know you're fine." And she hit me again.

I sat up. We were somewhere dark. There was no Ian, no Watlin, no Guards, no anybody else. Just me and Jess. Me and Jess and Raphael Michaud. I was atop something acutely uncomfortable. It turned out to be the grease-clotted gears of the building's elevator, cables rising above my head into an endless square of darkness.

"I'm sorry, *mon frere*," said Michaud. "I though the elevator car was below you."

That was bullshit. He'd known the car was above because the improvised fire bomb had to be down here, and its explosion needed to be visible from above. Not that landing atop the car's roof instead of the basement gears would have hurt any less.

I climbed down. I'd hit the motor hard enough that some of my bones had wedged in nooks and crannies. I had to pull very hard to extricate myself, and the pulling broke my bones again. I fell off more than anything orderly, then laid there until I'd healed. The aftertaste of acute pain was like a haze. Even after it was gone, it seemed to endure in memory.

"Are the Guards gone?"

"*Oui,*" said Michaud. "They saw the flames after you took a stake they believed to be through the heart. After I told them you were dead, that was enough. If they'd stayed longer, I'd only have asked them to help clean."

I rubbed my chest. There'd always been the chance that Raphael's grasp of anatomy might be off or that he'd turn out to have crappy aim. When we'd sent our message to Ian's maker through Ian's blood, we'd done our best to suggest hints for faking my death and avoiding my real death. Among those: consulting an encyclopedia for the location of the heart. Of course he hadn't had a set here, so he'd made a guess. Lucky for me, he'd guessed well. That'd been real wood inside me, and it couldn't have missed my heart by more than an inch.

I sat up again, this time healed and as well as a vampire could expect to be after all we'd been through. "You didn't have to hit me so hard," I said.

"I know I didn't."

"And you," I said to Jess, "didn't have to hit me at all."

"You had it coming."

They traded a glance. Michaud wasn't one to share smiles with humans, or really to smile at all. Still, the glance weighed tons. They'd both hated me. I guess now, after all that punishment, we were even enough.

"Ask you something?" I said.

"*Oui.*"

"You could have really killed me."

"That's not a question," Raphael said.

"If Leigh really had evidence, then you know what I did. François didn't follow me to America. I stole him away. You had all the right in the world to take revenge ... and all the opportunity, with those Guards as backup."

Jess almost put a hand on my shoulder. I guess I was square with her, because talk of accepting death made her uncomfortable. She pulled it back, but I'd already seen the gesture.

"We'd made a deal," Raphael answered. "You told me what Leigh was trying to do in your message through Adam, and in turn I agreed to forgive you."

"You didn't need to keep the deal," I said. "You knew what you needed to know, but you could have disposed of me, too. Orchestrating a fight, having your guys plant home-made napalm down here ... it's hardly worth it."

"Would you rather I'd killed you?"

"I just wonder, is all. There was a moment after you stabbed me that I thought you'd changed your mind."

He smiled in that superior way of his. "But that is the difference between us," he said. "I may take what I want, but I will never break my word."

Somehow, that stung a lot more than being stabbed through the lungs. I didn't respond. There was no good answer to what had proven unquestionably true.

I looked up the shaft. Another thing I knew about Michaud was that even when he was feeling amiable, he had an accountant's sense of righting the ledger. I may have informed him about a poison pill in his midst, but snitching on Leigh hadn't bought me free reign to destroy his build-ing. We'd bashed up the stairwell, broken walls, and blown a showy little bomb to mimic my body going up in fire — a bomb that may, who knew, have damaged the elevator's works. There'd be bills to pay, damage for me to have fixed. Even with his friends, which I hadn't been for a long time, he kept score.

"I guess I should consider myself lucky," I said.

"*Absolument.* Although I do wonder what will happen when the Council learns you are not dead."

I wondered that, too. But the Vampire Council was, above all things, officious and lazy. The sheer volume of officiousness involved in vampire law, though, made it easy to be lazy. Why would they come after me later, if they'd already filed the paperwork to close my case? If Raphael didn't make a stink, I imagined they'd let it go. Today, due to ceremony, the Guards had been bound to protect the verdict rather than admit their judgment had been wrong. Tomorrow? It was hard to believe they'd care.

I paced the sub-basement. It was just the three of us.

"You're in the cellar," I told Michaud.

"I had to see if you'd lived, or if I'd managed to kill you."

"But what about the spiders?"

He shrugged. Maybe this was the beginning of something new for Raphael Michaud.

"The Council Guard glamoured our friends," Jess said. "Watlin is now confused and totally incomprensible — so basically, the way he usually is. Ian's hiding in the wine cellar until the sun goes down."

"And you?"

"Your preemptive counter-glamour on me worked a treat. I just tried to look vacant-eyed until they left in their blacked-out bus and Ian let me back in through the loading dock."

"So you remember everything?"

"I remember you lying to me. To all of us. The others still know you're a vampire, by the way. Sally, Danno ..."

"They won't remember for long," I said. They had until nightfall, at which point I'd need to head back to the squat and do some glamouring of my own. It was for their own good, forgetting what they'd seen and heard. I'd just be Maurice again: a kid with a weird allergy to sunlight.

"I will," said Jess.

I waited to see if she'd express a preference. If she didn't want the burden of knowledge, I could make her forget. If she wanted to keep what she'd learned, however, I wasn't going to take it away. She still had unresolved questions about her mother. Assuming she wanted it, I figured she'd earned whatever hows and whys other vampires could give her.

There was a commotion. We looked up as Leigh entered followed by all six of Michaud's red-suspendered yes-men. She saw Michaud and paced forward, new vampirism turning her movements catlike. She had magnetism now that she hadn't had before, and I was glad Anarchy Jim and Roland weren't here to see it. They'd boner up. That's how those perverts were.

Her face was all business. She looked like she had a grievance — not with her boss, but with the general state of affairs. The situation had rocked the building and caused a construction nightmare, and as Michaud's right hand, she'd be the one to deal with it..

Except that shortly after seeing Michaud, she saw me and Jess.

She gasped, blinking.

"He's alive," she said, speaking of me.

"Regrettably," said Michaud.

"Are you ... Why aren't you restraining him?"

"Because I am not a policeman."

"But he—"

"I know what he did, *mon cheri*. But Adam has also informed me what *you* did."

"I didn't do anything. And Adam?" She looked at the hawk-faced man: Ian's maker and the spy she'd used to observe us, through Ian, all along. "Adam doesn't know anything."

"Perhaps. How is your transformation?"

"*What?*" The least relevant of things. She seemed unable to believe I was unstaked, that nobody was chasing me with one right now.

"I asked if you are yet vampire, or still mostly human."

"I'm ... *Why?*"

She was trying to stand proud despite the surprise, assuming the authority of the Council and her recently filed Graduation would back her up. But she was new to our world. She didn't know that unless it had a very good reason to care, the Council was a straw man.

The word that came out of Michaud's mouth next was a jumble of phonics and sibilants — a mishmash of a dozen languages. It was a word I'd mostly forgotten the trick of — the word that unlocked the vessel that had once resided in François's mind.

Then he said, "At what age did Clarence d'Volia father his first illegitimate child?"

Leigh answered as if Raphael had pulled her string. It came out of her without volition, the way a *tasse débordante* is supposed to dispense its information.

"Fifteen, in 1866. The first of three before he turned eighteen." When the words stopped, Leigh slapped her hand over her mouth. Too late. She'd already proven what needed proving.

"As I figured." He turned to me. "Maurice? We should mitigate."

"No," Leigh said. She looked pale. She'd studied the way of *tasses débordante* extensively in preparation for becoming one. She knew what "mitigate" meant. In order to mitigate a vessel, all keyholders have to agree ... and that, especially following the intended death of at least one of us, wasn't something Leigh had planned on happening.

I looked at Raphael. He looked at me. We said the mitigation word together, then watched Leigh's face as the buried mnemonic trigger did its work. All she'd stored in her synapses was being methodically erased, turning her into a vessel no more — and what a waste, she must have thought, considering how close she'd been to fully vampire ... how close she'd been to being able to unlock it herself using the key in Raphael's blood.

When it was done, she stood there vacant. Just an ordinary woman now, still days away from being an ordinary creature of the night.

"You would have had Maurice kill me, *n'est-ce pas?*"

Leigh didn't answer. He went on.

"But *of course* you would have had him kill me. Who else could? Who else had reason?" Raphael laughed — good humor for someone who'd come so close to overthrow. "I have not had time to talk much with my old friend on these matters, but Adam has shared with me what he saw through the man Ian's eyes and what you asked him to do. Perhaps you're unaware it's considered illegal to use blood ties for the purpose of spying? Such is the way of things. But these are concepts you must learn, along with it being inadvisable to stage a *coup* against a man such as me."

"I didn't—!"

He waved at her. "No, no, *of course* you didn't. You

would not be so foolish as to put yourself front and center. But if Maurice had managed to kill me, as he by all rights would have if we hadn't reached an agreement, would you not have taken my place?"

"I ... I ..."

"But of course you would have. It would only be right. And as a self-aware *tasse débordante?* Well, you might have been formidable. But, alas. It was not to be."

He snapped his fingers above his head. The six vampire yes-men stood tall to comply. They took the hint, grabbing Leigh's arms.

"Are you going to kill me?" she asked.

"Worse, my love. I going to fire you."

"What about Adam?" she shouted as they dragged her toward the stairs. "Adam worked with me! He turned that kid and helped me spy! *He betrayed you!*"

"So sad, to see the drowning attempt to bring others down with them," Michaud said, fussily adjusting cuffs caked with gore. "Adam and I made a deal. Maurice told Adam, through Ian, that he would be well-rewarded if he brought me news of your duplicity. I said that I would forgive him, as I am a forgiving man, so long as he showed loyalty when it mattered."

"Adam," Leigh said, glaring at the hawk-faced vampire, "is not bought with loyalty."

"True. That is why we agreed to give him your job, now that it is vacant and I am in need of a someone as ruthless as me ... but not quite as ruthless as you."

He snapped again, giving the utmost of European "take her from my sight" gestures. The vampires dragged her up the stairs, shouting for revenge.

"You won't hurt her?" Jess asked Michaud when she was gone.

"Would it bother you if I did?"

Jess looked at me as if for the answer. Michaud went on without her response.

"I have *already* hurt her," he said.

And with another of those very European waves, the matter was dismissed.

THIRTY-FOUR
DOGSHIT

Four weeks later, after life had mostly gone back to normal and nobody but Jess recalled what had happened, we found something tacked to the front door of the squat. At first I thought it was an eviction notice, but it turned out to be an envelope with several folded papers inside.

The topmost was a note:

It is a piece of dogshit. You may have it in good health.
RM

Behind the note was a quitclaim deed for the parcel that held the Whiskey Dick. We'd already gotten word that the squat was to be torn down, which by that point I was actually fine with. We'd known since the day after the fight at the Fleur-de-Lis building that Raphael planned to build an apartment building on this spot. The block across the street, however, was apparently on uncertain ground. The single time I'd spoken with Raphael after our near-death fight (and, as it turned out, the last time I've spoken with him since), he'd told me the whole thing was giving him headaches worth a truckload of *mon dieu*. The Dick in particular wasn't even worth its land value. There was a sinkhole beneath it or something. Apparently deeding it away was his way of solving the problem, erasing his burden for the property taxes.

Jess was reading over my shoulder. We'd sneaked away to look at the envelope's contents since none of the other punks knew what we'd done — or consequently why the power behind Fleur-de-Lis would suddenly have a change of heart.

"He gave you the Whiskey Dick?"

I scanned the deed. "Actually, he gave *you* the Whiskey Dick."

She snatched the paper from my hand. Her eyes showed disbelief. When she got to where her name had been entered, though, her eyes began to well. I saw it, looked at the deed, and didn't understand. Jess wasn't the type to be touched by generosity. She'd been hardened by the street, and saw most generous things as simply what she was due.

"What is it?"

"My name." She tapped the paper.

I read: "'Jessica Elaine Dormer.' So?"

"My middle name is Leslie."

"I guess he got it wrong."

"Elaine was my mother's name," she said.

I wasn't sure how to respond to that. If Michaud had done that on purpose — something that sounded very un-Michaud, though he'd already proven he could surprise me — I wasn't even sure how. I may still have had a few drops of Ian's blood in me when we'd spoken. I suppose it's possible that the connection from me to Ian to Adam had uncovered that particular bit of miscellany: Jess's mother, whose name

I may have heard when she'd told her story, picked up by Michaud as surprising tribute — or even as atonement on behalf of his kind. Also not like Michaud at all. But it'd been sixty years since we'd parted, and it was possible that even though I hadn't remembered the name, he'd plucked it out. It was possible that even after a hundred years of rocky, back-stabbing, murderous friendship, people could change.

It gave me heart. Not for Michaud, but for myself.

I left Jess with the deed. In the lead-up to our eviction from the squat, most of my punk rock friends had already found new homes — or, in many cases, simply gone back to their current ones. Roland, Sally, and Danno had moved back in with their parents. Watlin, by all accounts, had vanished. Anarchy Jim and Stacy Grace had hooked up in a surprising turn of events and gotten a run-down apartment together — an interesting twist, seeing as Jim had apparently been squirreling money away all along. We hadn't seen Drag Worm Ian; word was he'd moved out of the sewer and back into his Lakeway home, blacking out his room and pretending to be moody. But through all of it, I hadn't stopped wondering about Jess. With the squat on the chopping block, I'd already decided to move on. Recent events had shaken me, and in the wake I'd changed my wardrobe without even meaning to. I was back to plain shirts, plain shoes, plain old boring Maurice hair. I looked normal — not punk at all. As it maybe should have been all along.

But Jess? Well, now it looked like she'd have a home after all, assuming she didn't mind sleeping on the lower floor of a club that smelled like beer and puke. The Whiskey Dick, unlike the squat, hadn't been abandoned by the usual crowd. It'd stayed open in the lead-up to its demolition date, then stayed open longer when the demolition hadn't happened. Now it might stay open for decades, even if it was falling down. Take *that*, gentrification! And in that pile of dogshit, as Michaud had called it, my friends could still be together.

It was after dusk. Intuition told me to go for a walk, to leave Jess more or less alone with only Hardcore Sally passed out in the kitchen. Instead, I stopped at the pay phone. I had a quarter I didn't remember grabbing, as if I'd planned to come here all along.

I dialed. I asked for the operator, then gave a number and reversed the charges.

"Hello?" came a familiar, sorely missed voice.

"Celeste? It's Maurice."

There was a long pause. In that pause, she was probably considering all the unkind, totally justified things she could say to me. But I've been with my wife for nearly a thousand years, and in that time she's learned that the most important things are sometimes unsaid.

Finally she spoke.

"Are you ready to come home?"

I looked back at the squat. I looked at the block next door, to the caving-in roof of the club where we'd spent so many nights. They were the same buildings, but they struck me as somehow changed. They were sepia toned under the dim streetlights, as if this slice of life had already become an old memory.

At the corner, one of Anarchy Jim's too-on-the-nose subvertisements remained. It was a bus stop poster of Dolly Parton bearing the legend:

You're home in Austin!

Below it, Jim had spraypainted:

So fuck off and go away!

It was, in its stupid way, fitting.

"Yes," I told Celeste. "I'm ready to come home."

I don't remember what we said after that. In the end, it didn't matter.

THIRTY-FIVE
NEXT TIME

Annabel touched her cheek. Was she crying? That didn't even make sense.

Maurice looked up. She swiped the tear, blinked as if no big deal, and crossed her legs.

"So Raphael just let you go?" she asked.

Maurice shrugged. "There was no reason not to. If he'd had a change of heart and gone to the Council again, they'd have investigated and uncovered his part in faking my death. They found out soon enough anyway, and as I figured, Logan and the Council just let it go. Not the last time I'd get in trouble with the Council. I mean, even now, with Reginald—"

Annabel sensed a distraction and cut him off.

"What about Leigh?"

"She went off. Was a vampire. Whatever other vampires do, I suppose she did it."

"But she tried to kill you both."

"Actually, she tried to get *me* to kill Raphael, after which the *Council Guard* was supposed to kill me. Adam, who took over her job, was supposed to keep his mouth shut because he'd been an accomplice, and after glamouring the humans and disposing of Ian as wanton creation, there'd be nobody left. She was a manipulator, not a fighter. Take away her toys and she's harmless. Well. As harmless as any vampire, I mean."

"And the vessel? The *tasse?*"

"Decimated."

"She couldn't access it?"

"It no longer existed. It was erased when we mitigated it, like formatting a hard drive."

Annabel bobbed her head, letting it all settle and make sense. She gave the room a moment to breathe, refusing to look at the clock lest it rush him. It was late; that was all she cared to know. Her husband would be waiting for her, but seeing as he sucked, she didn't care about that, either.

Thought of him made something change inside Annabel, though. She blinked, hearing urges, pushing down a voice that wanted to speak. As her will was weakening — as that odd sense inside her was just starting to rise again with new questions and new directions — Maurice broke the silence.

"So what do you think?" he asked.

"About what?"

"Am I still deflecting?"

"Well, no. But ..."

"You said I was deflecting. You said I couldn't face myself, so I was turning stuff around on you."

"You were. But then you came clean." She shifted. "Tell me, and try to be honest. When you began telling me this story, did you plan to hide the fact that you'd once been like Michaud — that even after feuding with him, you'd again become his friend?"

Maurice considered. "Maybe."

"What about the fact that you didn't just leave and go to America, but instead stole François to go with you?"

"Well ..."

"Or that the wine you told me all about was already gone?"

He shrugged. "I don't know *what* I thought."

"How could you have told the story without the truth, Maurice? I'm not asking in a judgmental way. I mean it literally. The story falls apart without those details. It can't even end, because you couldn't have told me about your friends' discovery that the wine didn't exist and that you'd really been looking for François."

He seemed to think. "I guess I didn't consider that."

"The story couldn't have been told if you'd continued lying to me. It's just not possible."

"I guess that's why you wormed the truth out of me."

"I did," Annabel said, "but you were the one who started telling an unfinishable story. Is it possible that you *wanted* to get called out? Isn't it possible that the reason you told me this story in the first place is because you *meant* for me to catch you, and make you tell it with all its warts?"

"Hmm. Maybe."

"Do you feel better?'

He took a moment. "Actually, I do."

"Then maybe you *are* getting better."

He had nothing to say to that. The room was silent.

"I guess that's enough for today," Annabel finally said. She looked at the clock and added, "*Really* enough for today."

Maurice looked too. "Shit. I'm so sorry. I just go on and on."

"It's okay. I *let* you go on and on."

"Same time next week?"

"Same time," Annabel said.

He stood. He opened his mouth. The voice of Annabel's husband, inside her and greedily curious, seemed to sit up and pay attention.

"Next time I'm here," Maurice said, "Ask me about my trip to Chicago. The first one, in 1892."

"Why?"

"Because it was another lie. I told you last visit that when I went to New York in the 1920s, that it was my first trip."

"And you want to explore your lies?"

"I'd like to get out of the habit of telling them. How's *that* for personal growth, Doctor?" Then he smiled. So hard to think of him as a creature.

"Bye, then," he said. And was gone.

When the office was again quiet, Annabel plucked her phone from her purse. The presence inside of her seemed to move away, now personified on the connection's other end. She carried two copies of her husband with her: the one inside, which she knew about while also not knowing was there at all, and this other one — the real one — who was back at home, waiting to be synched with his psychic twin.

"Wath it a good appointment?" he asked, with his lisp.

"It was," Annabel said. She was feeling less herself than usual — something that seemed typical after sessions with Maurice. She couldn't help feeling like Maurice had felt, in his story. He'd come to realize his life had been manipulated behind the scenes by Leigh Everness — and for Annabel, the same feeling came from her own life, from her marriage, from her relationship with this strange, strange man. "I'll tell you all about it when I get home," she said.

She felt swimmy. Almost hypnotized. Hadn't she felt

this way before? If so, why did she always forget when it was over?

She was about to hang up when she remembered something.

"Before he left," Annabel told her husband, "he said I should ask him next time about the fair."

"What fair?"

"Chicago. End of the 1800s."

Silence on the other end. Then: "Did he mention a man? A man named Holmth?" She translated his speech impediment: *A man named Holmes.*

Annabel thought. She wasn't sure, but she didn't think so. She said as much.

"Come home and tell me everything," he said.

She hung up. She would do as he said. She always did.

Unbidden, she thought of Daisy, Maurice's late vampire daughter. Why would she think of Daisy, in association with her husband?

Her blood seemed to churn. To rise up.

But then it was gone, and she was just Annabel again.

THE END

ALSO BY JOHNNY B. TRUANT

Winter Break

Pattern Black

Pretty Killer

Cursed

The Bialy Pimps

Namaste

The Target

La Fleur de Blanc

Axis of Aaron

Devil May Care

Screenplay

The Island

Burnout

Sick and Wired

UNICORN WESTERN:

Unicorn Western

The Wanderers

A Fistful of Magic

Shimmer to Yuma

The Man Who Shot Alan Whitney

The Spectacular Seven

Resurrection

Save the City

Save the Girl

Save the World

Longshot

THE INEVITABLE:

Robot Proletariat

The Infinite Loop

The Hard Reset

Cascade Failure

Reboot

En3my

DEAD CITY:

Dead City

Dead Nation

Dead Planet

Dead Zero

Empty Nest

THE DREAM ENGINE:

The Dream Engine

The Nightmare Factory

The Ruby Room

The Pandora Core

The Engine Convergence

The Tinkerer's Mainspring

GORE POINT:

Gore Point 1

Gore Point 2

Gore Point 3

THE BEAM:

The Beam: Season One

The Beam: Season Two

The Beam: Season Three

The Beam Season Four

The Beam Season Five

Future Proof

Plugged

The Future of Sex

THE TOMORROW GENE:

The Tomorrow Gene

The Eden Experiment

The Tomorrow Clone

Null Identity

COMEDIES:

Everyone Gets Divorced

Greens

Fiends

Decoy Wallet

NONFICTION:

The Fiction Formula

Fiction Unboxed

Iterate & Optimize

The Story Solution

Write. Publish. Repeat.

The One With All the Writing Advice